The Salvation of Yasch Siemens

THE SALVATION OF YASCH SIEMENS

Armin Wiebe

TURNSTONE PRESS 1984

Turnstone Press
607-100 Arthur Street
Winnipeg, Manitoba
Canada R3B 1H3

Turnstone Press gratefully acknowledges the assistance
of the Canada Council and the Manitoba Arts Council.

Design: Steven Rosenberg

This book was typeset by B/W Type Service Ltd.
and printed by Hignell Printing Limited.

Printed in Canada.
Sixth printing: January, 1993

Canadian Cataloguing in Publication Data

Wiebe, Armin
Salvation of Yasch Siemens

ISBN 0-88801-084-2

I. Title.
PS8595.I32S3 1984   C813'.54   C84-091128-9
PR9199.3.W53S3 1984

For the Riverview writers
who laughed first
and for Millie
who let me write.

"My God, how we adored this buggering up of our lovely language for we felt that all languages were lifeless if not buggered up a little."

Josef Skvorecky, "Red Music"

Chapter One

The year they built the TV tower I was heista kopp in love with Shaftich Shreeda's daughter, Fleeda. I was only almost sixteen and Fleeda was almost sixteen, too, and I had been in love with her all the way since we were only almost fourteen when she looked at me in her little pocket mirror from where she was sitting in the next row in school and I just went heista kopp in love. And now we were both almost sixteen and everything should have fit together real nice, only when you are almost sixteen the whole world seems to get in the way of things that you want because when you are only almost sixteen you don't have a driver's licence. That's where the puzzle doesn't fit. That's how come the weeds grow in the garden.

I mean, me and Fleeda were going pretty good. Like I walked with her home from choir practice three times, and one Sunday after dinner when I knew that her brothers weren't at home I went to visit her and we went for a walk down to the

1

big ditch that cuts us off from the States. The new TV tower was there on the States side and we talked about how scary it would be to have to climb all the way to the top to screw in a new light bulb and we talked about some of the funny things people said when they were first building the tower. Like some said you wouldn't even have to buy a TV because the tower was so close that all you would need would be rabbit ears with a white cloth hanging over it and you would be able to see the picture. Others said that they were going to put a big ball at the top of the tower with a helicopter, and some said no, they would put big mirrors on the top because with TV you had to have mirrors because of the picture. And so some right away said that if you wanted to watch the TV you would just need to line a mirror up with the tower and you would be able to see it.

Fleeda and me laughered ourselves over these stories and I was feeling pretty good and was sneaking my hand close to Fleeda's so that I could maybe hold it a little bit because when you are heista kopp in love you should hold hands with a girl. But when my finger touched her hand just a little bit she said she would have to go back home because her mom and dad were going to visit some cousins and she wanted to go with. So we walked back to her place and I didn't try to take her hand but I was still feeling okay and I was thinking that I would come back the next Sunday in the evening because it is maybe easier to do such things in the evening. But when I did the next Sunday, Fleeda was not home and then after I found out that she had gone to the Neche show with some shluhdenz from Altbergthal and I mean I was feemaesich mad over that, but what can you do when you are only almost sixteen?

Then the next Sunday in Sunday School, Shtemm Gaufel Friesen had the nerve to say that girls mature faster than boys and the girls all sat there with their noses just a little bit higher and I thought, that's just what we need for girls to hear and they will all be going out with grandfathers like that shluhdenz from

2

Altbergthal who is seventeen or eighteen or nineteen even. Something must be wrong with such old fortzes that they can't pick up girls their own age. Mature faster! Shtemm Gaufel must think that girls are like grain or something that he talks about maturing faster. It's just something else against you when you are only almost sixteen. Why can't the world do nothing right and let people hang around with their own age?

Well, even when you are heista kopp in love and floating in a sea of heartbreak your Muttachi still makes you stand up in the morning and go to weed beets by Yut Yut Leeven's place. And on the beetfield I make the time seem not so long by pointing my eyes all the time to Shtramel Stoezs's long legs that are sticking out from her blue jeans that are cut off quite high from the knee and are getting burned in nice and brown from the sun, and it seems like if I let myself I could fall into love with her quite easy, even if she is sixteen already. But come to me baby I'm a one-woman man. Still it's nice to have Shtramel weeding in front of me in the next row and if I don't look at Shtramel I can look at her sister Shups, who is fourteen only and her legs are shorter but they are so nice and smooth and have more curve than Shtramel's and if I was a cradle robber I could let myself fall into love with her, too. But I say to myself that I'm only practicing looking for Fleeda, and that even if the Stoezs girls have nice legs, for sure they couldn't be so nice as Fleeda's even if I have only seen Fleeda's up to her knees when she has a dress on in church. A man needs a woman his own age and that is Fleeda Shreeda. But the Stoezs girls are nice to have on a beetfield.

So anyways on Sundays after dinner Hova Jake usually picks me up. Hova Jake is only almost sixteen, too, but he has this grandfather that's ninety years old and can't drive his own car any more, so Hova Jake drives it for him and they come to pick me up and we go looking at the crops, me in the back seat and Hova behind the steer and the grandfather sitting on the

3

woman's side looking out the window and knacking sunflower seeds or sucking on his cigarette holder. And it sure is exciting riding around in the back seat with Hova Jake singing while he drives because the old Plymouth doesn't even have a radio and the old grandfather is singing his own song in Flat German or Russian and qwauleming smoke from his cigarette. It is a terrible thrill to ride around like that but it is better than staying home and playing catch with yourself.

Then one Sunday Hova Jake comes on Sunday evening to pick me up and his grandfather isn't with and Hova says, "C'mon Yasch, let's take some girls along." My heart starts to clapper real fast and I think maybe I should go to the beckhouse but I creep in the car and as we drive along I ask Hova, "Well, which girls do you want to take with?" and he says, "Let's see if Fleeda Shreeda is at home." And my heart clappering speeds up so much I think it will bounce right through my ribs but I say, "Well for sure." I start to wonder right away whose she will be if she comes along and I wish I had smeared on some of Futtachi's green Rawleigh shaving lotion after I did the chores, but it's too late now because I can see Shaftich Shreeda's place already. And I am hoping that Fleeda is at home and I am hoping that Fleeda isn't at home and I am terribly scared that if she is at home she will say no and I am terribly scared that she will say yes to Hova Jake and I am scared too that she will say yes to me. And I wonder if Hova Jake is scared, too, but I sure can't say what he feels because he is humming "Just as I am without one plea" and I wish there was a radio in the car because listening is easier than talking.

"Are you going to talk?" Hova asks when he slows down by Shaftich Shreeda's driveway, and before I know what I'm saying my mouth says, "Sure, okay" and then my heart clappers a hundred miles an hour. Then there is Fleeda sitting on the porch steps playing with a cat and she has her hair in rollers and she is wearing short pants with no shoes. Hova honks his horn.

Fleeda looks at us but she doesn't stand up. And I wonder me a little how come she would have her hair in curlers on a Sunday evening. "Hello Fleeda," I say, almost steady. "Want to...."

"Joe isn't home," she calls. "He went to Mouse Lake." Joe is her brother and I don't even like him so what the dukkat is she talking about him for? I am quiet for a minute, then I say, "Want to go for a ride?" Fleeda looks at us, then she looks to the barn. She stands up, starts to walk to the car, the cat in her arms, but she is wiggling her whole body just a little as she walks and for an eyeblink it almost seems like her legs are a bit lumpy and bowlegged and for sure far whiter than the Stoezs sisters' but that's only for an eyeblink and then she is perfect again, even with rollers in her hair, and I wish she would put the cat down so I could see everything when she walks and she is all the time looking to the barn like she is watching out for something. Then Hova Jake sticks his head past me and says, "Want to go for a ride?" Fleeda tilts her head sideways a bit and she looks us on with her eyes almost closed. She chews her gum a bit.

"Can't," she says.

"How come not?" I ask.

"Grounded."

"How come?" Hova says.

"Came home too late last night."

"Fleeda, get back in the house!"

Fleeda jerks around like a bee bit her and she runs in the house. We turn and see Shaftich Shreeda walking from the barn with two pails of milk but even then his overalls are wiggling back and forth like when a dog is wagging his tail. But it is easy to see that Shreeda isn't shaftich today. Hova starts to drive away and he says "Shit" under his breath but I am thinking in my head that maybe it's not so bad because if Fleeda is grounded she can't go with that shluhdenz from Altbergthal neither and I am thinking that it would have been maybe a good time to go visiting on foot and I could have sat on the step with Fleeda and played with the cat. But it's too late for that now and I am wondering if Fleeda is grounded for a long time. And I am wondering so much to myself that I don't notice that Hova has held the car still again.

"Get in the back." Hova is opening the door for Shtramel Stoezs. Her sister Shups is there, too, and I know that Jake wants me to get in the back with her. Well, it's not like I'm scared of Shups or nothing like that because we weed beets together. It's just that I'm a one-woman man and what will Fleeda think about this and for an eyeblink I think maybe she wouldn't give a damn, but I wipe that away real fast. I open the door for Shups and she slides in the back seat and I slide in after her and everybody is talking real easy and I am thinking that maybe riding with Shups in the back seat will be good practice so I know what to do when I get my driver's licence and I take Shaftich Shreeda's daughter Fleeda along.

The time goes quite quickly. We have so many things to talk about because we weed beets on the same field and the smell from the clover fields is nice and I can smell some perfume from Shups even if she is sitting almost on the other side of the car. It gets a little darker and we are driving slowly through a lot of field roads because we can't go to town without a driver's licence. Shtramel just has her learner's even if she is already sixteen. Hova Jake sings lots of songs because the car doesn't have a radio. Soon we are driving through some trees and there are no farmers for some miles around and it is getting a little bit darker and I see that Shtramel is slipping herself closer to Hova Jake and I look at Shups and she smiles at me. The moon is coming up and I move a little bit closer to Shups and then Hova is driving along the road beside the ditch that cuts us off from the States. He holds still there for a while and we can see the lights on the TV tower blinking on and off. I think about the talk I had with Fleeda about it and I look at Shups and she has slipped a little bit closer to me. I carefully reach out my hand to hers and I wish my hand wasn't so wet and I wish I had some shaving lotion on because it seems like I can smell the barn a little bit but Shups is holding my hand and then I only smell her perfume and I almost forget about Fleeda Shreeda there in the moonshine in the car where we can see the TV lights blinking off and on. In the front seat Hova Jake is sitting real close to Shtramel but he doesn't do much neither. They just talk and laugh a lot and then all of a sudden Shtramel says that it's time to go home. We drive home slowly and I hold Shups's hand all the way and think this is sure good practice.

Next day on the beetfield Shups and Shtramel are real friendly, only not so friendly that the Leeven boys have anything to tease me with. Most of the time I can be quiet and look at the sisters' legs and think about Fleeda Shreeda. Then in the evening when it is almost dark and all the chores are finished I go walking down the road to Fleeda's place, just dreaming that maybe she will be walking alone, too. It would be nice to walk to the boundary ditch and stand there in the dark while the TV tower lights blink on and off and I forget that before I can get all the way to Fleeda's place I have to go past Shtramel and Shups's place, and really I am walking in my head more than on the road when all of a sudden I hear somebody say, "Who's that bum?" and I turn to look and there are Shtramel and Shups standing by their driveway. "Hallelujah, I'm a bum," I say. They laugh and come walk beside me.

We walk along the road to the States, past Fleeda's place, and I try to look at the window in the house that I think is Fleeda's without letting the girls notice it. When we are past about a quarter mile we see somebody walking toward us and soon I can see that it is Fleeda, alone. In my head I am swearing at the Stoezs girls and why did they have to come with tonight when here would have been my big chance, but I mean, two's company and three's a crowd. What can I do now except try not to let my eyes fall out while the girls stop to talk to Fleeda.

Fleeda wants to know if they are walking their dog. Shtramel laughs and says "Yes" and Fleeda wants to know where they found such a mutt. Then Fleeda says she better go home and tells the Stoezs girls not to fight over who will play with the dog. We all laugh again and I am sure glad that it's night time because for sure my face must be real red.

So I walk farther with Shtramel and Shups when all of a sudden Shtramel says, "Oh, I have to ask Fleeda something," and she turns and runs back and I am left with Shups and we walk alone a little while and don't say anything, but it feels real nice because it is warm and there is a little bit of wind, just enough to blow the mosquitoes away. The TV tower is blinking off and on and there is a slice of moon in the sky. I ask Shups if she ever went all the way to the tower and she says no and I can feel she has moved a little closer to me, so I tell her about the time me and Hingst Heinrichs went across the boundary all the way to the tower and there was a guy working there, just sitting in the little shack under the tower, watching a TV that was built right into a workbench and there were lots of knobs and things. We talked with him a little bit and he said we should watch out for the border patrol and we thought it was pretty funny how the States people are always so full of police stuff and everything, but we didn't stay long because he was finished his shift and he wanted to go home to Pembina where he lived. And while I am telling Shups all this, she is listening quietly and her hand touches mine, sometimes accidentally on purpose, and after she has done this three times I catch it in mine and we walk along the boundary ditch.

We stop walking when we're even with the tower and I almost say, "Let's go all the way to the tower," but I think well maybe it's too late already and Shups is only fourteen and besides I should maybe save going to the tower for sometime when I'm with Fleeda. I mean, this walking around with Shups is just practice I figure.

8

"Let's sit down a little bit," I say and we do. I let the tower blink five times, then I put my arm around her and she leans her head on my shoulder and we watch the tower blink, talk about the beetfield and things that happened in school last year, and she laughs when I say a joke and she smells like clover and earth and Camay soap and I am trying to gribble out if I should kiss her or not. I mean how is a guy to know exactly how to do it, like the Danny Orlis books for sure don't say how and the Sunday School leaflets talked about fondling breasts one time, but they sure didn't say how to get from here to there and then Shups says she'll have to go home now. So I say, "Okay, but maybe next time we can go earlier so we would have time to go all the way to the tower," and Shups just giggles and says, "Maybe the border patrol will get us." I walk with my arm around her waist and it feels good and I forget to take my arm back when we walk past Fleeda Shreeda's place, but lucky nobody is looking.

When we stop by her driveway we don't want to say good night yet and I figure I should get all the practice I can so I whisper, "Shups," and she turns to me and I quickly lean over and give her a kiss on the lips. She doesn't slap me or nothing like they do on TV. She just stands there, then I say "Good night" and Shups runs to her house.

So I feel pretty good when I walk home, thinking I got lots of good practice. I turn around a few times, looking at the tower blinking behind me, and I think next time we'll go all the way to the tower. Then I stop dead in my tracks. I am thinking that I would go next time with Shups to the tower when I should be thinking I would go next time with Fleeda. I get a funny feeling that maybe Fleeda, now that she has gone riding around in cars with all those grandfathers from Puggefeld and Prachadarp, she maybe won't want to do stuff like go walking to the tower. I mean on Sunday when me and Hova Jake tried to pick her up it was like she was talking down her nose at us. And when she said she was grounded, I don't know, she sure didn't seem like the same girl that went for a walk with me that time on a Sunday afternoon.

I have to help Futtachi get a few loads of hay the next day so I don't see Shups and Shtramel on the beetfield, and they finish the field that day so I don't see the girls till Sunday after church when the Stoezs girls and Fleeda are standing on the church steps and Shups and Shtramel have on brand new white high heels and Fleeda is wearing brown open toes with a flat heel and it seems like the real Fleeda doesn't match up the Fleeda that I have in my head and I get all mixed up inside. Shups sees me and gives me a wink and I think, "Well, okay Fleeda if you want to go with grandfathers from those other darps well it's your own funeral." Then Fleeda holds her head a certain way and she is laughing about something and I fall heista kopp in love with her all over again.

The whole afternoon I lie on my bed listening to country songs on my red plastic radio and I'm dreaming about Fleeda Shreeda and thinking I should have won that red convertible by the Morris Stampede and how it would be driving Fleeda around all over the country with a red convertible and all the farmers with their half-tons would be jealous. I wonder if she is still grounded yet and I fall asleep and dream that I am parked with Fleeda in the red convertible under the TV tower with the red lights blinking, only the red convertible has bucket seats and I think I can't have Fleeda sitting on the gear shift with her white dress and then Shups Stoezs climbs in between us and it doesn't bother her to sit on the gear shift. Then Fortz Funk from Puggefeld honks his horn on that old half-ton truck he has and Fleeda climbs out of the red convertible in her white dress and she doesn't even open the door, she just climbs over the side and creeps into Fortz Funk's truck and I see she gets some grease on her white dress and Muttachi calls me to come and eat faspa.

10

Hova Jake comes to pick me up again in the evening. His grandfather isn't along and Hova says he isn't feeling so good anymore, but he doesn't seem to worry himself over it. Hova doesn't even ask where we will go. He just drives straight to Stoezs's place to pick up the girls. From the way the girls are ready, it seems like Hova must have phoned them up to say he was coming. Well, Shups doesn't wait for it to get dark to slide closer to me on the seat. Hova drives on the field roads for a while, Shtramel sitting close to him and Shups close to me, and we sing some songs because there is no radio and we laugh a lot and by the time Hova stops the car by the big ditch and the tower is blinking there a half-mile over the border, I am holding Shups's hand in my wet palm and her leg inside her stretchy slacks is pressed against mine. Hova puts his arm around Shtramel and rubs his cheek against hers and Shups is leaning against me and I am a little nervous. So I whisper in her ear, "Let's go to the tower," and she says in my ear, "Okay." We crawl out of the car and Hova and Shtramel don't even notice when we leave.

The sunset is beautiful and we walk down into the ditch through the pepper bushes that grow there and up the other side and we are in the States. There is a strip of grass, then an alfalfa field with stacks of bales all over the field and then alfalfa smell mixes with Shups's perfume as we walk together holding hands. We look at the tower with two lights blinking and two lights on steady all the time and the light second from the top is burned out. The tower gets higher and higher as we come closer and we can see the white sections and the red sections even if it is starting to get dark. Then Shups trips on a clump of dirt and I reach for her with both arms so that she doesn't fall down and she is pressed against me and I feel her breasts through my shirt and her blouse. My heart pounds real fast and I hold her like that till she says, "We're not by the tower yet," so we walk closer with our arms around each other till we have to lean our heads back to see the top.

Shups slips away from me and runs to the bottom of the tower and it's not quite dark yet and I follow her and we can see the ladder that goes up the tower that they use to put new light bulbs in. And there is a sign that I can still read in the dark: DANGER DO NOT CLIMB. I look straight up the tower and from so close I can't even see the top lights blinking. The wind is shaking the tower just a little and I step closer to Shups and reach for her to give her a kiss and she wriggles away. "Catch me if you want to kiss me!" she yells and starts to climb the ladder.

"Hey, what are you doing? You're not supposed to climb up there."

"C'mon. Catch me and give me a kiss."

Shups is already ten rungs up the ladder. Well, shit, I figure, if she can climb up I can too. So I climb after her, looking all the time at the seat of her pants, thinking that that is maybe the only place I can kiss because there is hardly any room on the ladder. She climbs higher and higher quite fast and I follow, never looking down but I can't get closer to her. She is climbing as fast as I can, not slowing down at all, and the wind shakes the tower a little. I look down for the first time and it seems like I am just as high as a hydro pole already and Shups is ten rungs still higher. The sun going under is covered with clouds and it's getting pretty dark and when I look up again I can hardly see Shups above me. I climb higher even though now I feel like I need to piss, but I have to climb just as high as she does so I call, "How high are you going to go?" She answers, "To the first light or the second!"

I look past her to where the first light is blinking and it sure seems like a hartsoft long way yet. I climb up five more rungs and I can't see Shups anymore, it's too dark, and then I can't see the ground, just dark. All I can see is the red blinking light and some yardlights back in Canada and one car going along a road. I keep climbing. My arms are starting to get tired and the tower seems to shake each time I climb another rung and when I call to Shups again she doesn't say nothing and I get scared and think that maybe she fell off only I think if she fell off she would have screamed but maybe she was so scared that she couldn't even scream. So I call for her again and still she doesn't say nothing so I keep climbing and climbing and climbing and it is getting so dark I can hardly see my hands holding on the ladder in front of me and I'm feeling along the cold iron for each rung. I call for Shups again and listen and all I can hear is the wind and the wind seems terribly strong.

"Five steps more," I say to myself. And I pull myself up one, then two, three, then four and there is something just darker than dark and something lighter and I reach up and touch rubber and it is Shups's runner.

Shups giggles. "Boy, you are sure slow. I thought you'd want a kiss more than that."

I laugh a little and say, "I thought you were going up till the first light."

"Naw, who wants to kiss with a red light on!"

"So do I get my kiss now?"

"Okay, if you want to kiss my foot."

"Climb all the way up here just to kiss a foot? No way. I want more than that."

"Well then, you'll have to wait till we get down."

"Okay." I start down one rung.

"Yasch, wait."

"Okay, what?" Shups's shoes come down past my nose and I have to lean back a little to let her legs down between me and the ladder, then the seat of her pants is in front of my face and she says, "Yasch, hug me just a little bit." So I do it the best way I can, my head leaning into the seat of her pants and my arms around her legs and the ladder and I hold on as tight as I can and it feels good and starts to feel warm. "That's good, Yasch. Now I can climb down." Then I know that she is scared, too.

So we talk all the way down and it seems to take forever and when we stop to rest I put my hand on her leg or on her ankle that's bare between her shoe and her pantleg until she says, "Okay, now I can go again."

Some clouds move away from the half moon and when I look down I can see the tin roof of the little shack beside the tower, and it doesn't seem so terribly high any more and we climb down faster. But when our feet touch the ground our knees just bend like rubber and we fall down on the ground. I hear Shups's breathing beside me.

I raise myself up on my elbow and look at her lying there in the moonlight. Her eyes blink and they look wet. Shups sits up.

"You didn't kiss me yet," she says.

"I was just waiting for you to stop panting." I reach for her and I kiss her on the lips and squeeze her body to mine and she kisses me back and I don't think about it being practice for something else. I just do it because it is good to do right now and I think that it's good that when you are almost sixteen you don't have to climb all the way to the top of the tower. Then Shups says, "We better go back before the border patrol catches us." And I say, "Yeah, Shtramel and Hova Jake have probably smeared lipstick all over the car already." Shups gives me a poke. "Shtramel didn't have any lipstick on." So we walk back and when we can see the car already we turn and look at the tower blinking.

"How far do you think we climbed up?"

"Far enough," Shups says and she squeezes my hand.

Chapter Two

Brummtupp. Brummtupp. Rommelpot. Reibtrommel. Rubbeltrumm. The growling pot. The rubbing drum. Brumm. Brumm. Rummel. Rummel. Fortz. Fortz. Sylvesterabend. Brummtupp. Brummtupp. Sylvester's fart. Dummheit. Brummtupp. Brumm. Brumm. Rummel. Rummel. Sylvester. Sylvester the cat. Sylvester the catlicker. Brumm. Brumm. Dummheit. Muttachi said. Old dummheit from Russlaund. Russische dummheit. Brumm. Brumm. For sure it's dummheit to be in the box of a three-ton truck on New Year's Eve with a dress on and Muttachi's pink girdle and her size 49 brassiere full with two windballs. Dummheit. But Hova Jake said there had to be a woman along with the brummtupp. And I am the smallest so what could I do? And he said that the brummtupp had to ride in the cab because it wouldn't work right if it got too cold. Brummtupp. Sylvester. Why couldn't Sylvester be in the summer time?

Brrrrrummmmmmm. Thirty degrees below cold and a woman on the back of Hova Jake's three-ton. With Penzel Panna and Kunta Klassen. At least I didn't take my pants off like Laups Leeven wanted me to do. Laups Leeven in the front. In the cab. With Hingst Heinrichs and Hova Jake. And the brummtupp. Laups said he had to sit in the cab because he has a brummtupp too. Not a real one like Hova Jake's. No, just a night pail with a pig's bladder stretched over the top and he makes noise with a stick that he shoves in and out from a hole in the middle. Dummheit for sure. I mean, almost sixteen and dressed up like on Halloween when we were maybe nine years old or something. And the lipstick Hingst stole from his sister Kobbel tastes like crayons. But what can you do when you're only almost sixteen?

Besides, those other badels wouldn't have the nerves to put on a dress. Except Hova Jake and he has to play the brummtupp. His grandfather said a woman couldn't play the brummtupp. It just wouldn't be right. That's where Hova Jake learns everything from, his grandfather that's ninety years old. All about the olden days his grandfather tells him, how it was with the Flat Germans long ago in Russlaund and Dietschlaund and Hullaund right back to the time when everybody in the whole world was a Catlicker and prayed to Mary and paid money to the pope to be forgiven their sins. And Hova Jake sometimes tells us about these things when we're smoking on Sunday afternoons in Pracha Platt's barn. Sometimes if he gets excited he will have a smoke, too, though he goes to the Stookey House to school and they would kick him out if they found out that he smoked or fell in love. Only I think Hova Jake would be too smart for such a thing. If they smelled smoke on his clothes he would maybe tell them stories about some olden days' preachers who came here from Russlaund and liked to make their pipes qwaulem like a steam engine. But Hova Jake hardly ever smokes, only when you tell him he shouldn't or if he thinks it might bother

16

somebody. I don't know but it seems to me that Hova Jake will maybe be a preacher or a Bible school teacher when he is big and then maybe I will like to go to church too because with Hova Jake you sure don't go to sleep.

No sir, Hova Jake can make even the most boring thing exciting and it will seem like he has mixed the whole thing up but when it's over you wouldn't be able to blame anything wrong on Hova Jake. Like at the Stookey House where Hova is in grade eleven they have to take classes in Bible and stuff like that. So Hova writes essays about the Song of Solomon or one time he wrote a thing about dancing in the Bible and he couldn't even find one place where it said that dancing was bad. He talked about this with his grandfather, who said the Flat Germans used to dance, too, until some States preachers came to say that it was wrong. And another time for the Flat German history class Hova wrote an essay about some long-ago Flat Germans that figured to be really Christlich, people shouldn't have any clothes on.

Anyway it's a good thing Hova Jake didn't decide that we would do a play about those naked Flat Germans for the freiwilliges at the Sylvesterabend church. Sylvesterabend. Now why would the people call the New Year's Eve church after a cat in the comics? I wonder me that. I mean it makes about as much sense as going to church at all on New Year's Eve. In books and shows and things you hear about how people have parties and dances and things like that on New Year's Eve, but here in Gutenthal what do we have? We have Sylvesterabend. And that means church. Evening church like a Sunday Night Christian Endeavor. Only it's special, they say, because instead of telling people who will have to do things like sing songs or say up verses they have what they call freiwilliges. That means that anybody can go up and do something at the front. It sure is freewillingness all right, but not freewilling enough that a person can stay home from church and listen to the top country songs for the year on the radio. No sir, such freewillingness it doesn't give here around. And they don't leave the preacher to freewillingness neither. For sure they always have a preacher on New Year's Eve.

Now it wouldn't be so terribly bad if it was just a regular evening church which would be over soon and a person could get home in time to hear the top ten for the year at least. But no. After the church the older ones go home and the youth is supposed to stay behind for the Watch Night service. That means sitting on a church bench waiting for the clock to reach midnight. At least if you could go around and collect some New Year's kisses it would be worth waiting for. But it's only to listen to Shtemm Gaufel Friesen sing the first song and say the first prayer in the New Year. Sylvesterabend. Meow. But what can you do when you're only almost sixteen?

Well, I had already figured it out for myself that maybe the Watch Night service wouldn't be so bad if I could sit myself down so I could look the whole evening at Shtramel Stoezs or maybe Shaftich Shreeda's daughter Fleeda. Yeah, I could look them on for the whole evening and not get tired. And maybe Shtemm Gaufel Friesen would have one of his smart aleck ideas and try to have boys and girls sit together for a while. Sitting with one of those two would be alright—even if it's always hard to figure out something to say, when all that's in your head is words from country love songs.

But Hova Jake has figured something different for Sylvesterabend. The brummtupp. Like in the olden days, he said. His grandfather told him how to make one. Futtachi said something one time about a brummtupp and I wanted to know what it was and Muttachi hurry said it was just some dummheit from long ago.

It started Sunday after dinner before Sylvesterabend. And it seems like when you're only almost sixteen even the calendar is trying to nerk you and has made Sylvesterabend on a Monday.

That means you have to go to church on Sunday, two times, on Monday evening, and then yet on Tuesday morning because that's New Year's Day! I mean, it really makes a guy wonder what there could be in the world except church.

A bunch of us badels were smoking roll-your-owns in Pracha Platt's hayloft. Nobody lives at Pracha Platt's no more, but there is a good water hole there and we sometimes play hockey on the ice, only it was all full with snow and nobody brought a shovel along. So we went into the barn to see if we could find one, but we only found a manure fork. Kunta Klassen climbed up the ladder to the loft and we followed and there was lots of old junk but no shovel so Hingst brought out his Old Chum and Vogue papers and we all rolled ourselves a smoke.

So we were kicking at the old stuff, blowing smoke everywhere, and Penzel Panna and Laups Leeven found an old night pail and tried to make each other sit on it and I was thinking about Shtramel Stoezs and the little bit of a run she had by her knee in her stocking at Sunday School when all of a sudden we heard this loud fortzing noise from downstairs in the barn. Laups quickly held the night pail to Penzel's rear end: "Here use it already!" BRRRRUUUMMMM. BRRRRUUUMMMM. The fortzing was so loud the whole barn was echoing.

"It's Hova Jake!" Kunta Klassen said. He was looking through the ladder hole to the downstairs. The brumming stopped, the ladder squeaked and Kunta reached down for something.

"Hova, what have you here?" He is holding what looks like a nail barrel.

"Brummtupp."

"What?" We all went closer to look at this nail barrel that had one end covered with some leather. A long horse's tail was sticking out from the middle of the leather.

"It's a brummtupp. They used to use it on New Year's Eve. My grandfather told me all about it."

19

"What does it do?"

"Didn't you hear?"

"You mean that fortzing noise?"

"Yeah, let me show you." And Hova Jake grabbed the end of the horse tail in one hand and he started to rub it between his thumb and forefinger and that thing started to make that sound again. Brumm. Brumm. Rummel. Rummel. Fortz. Fortz. He rubbed faster and Laups said, "Pauss up that nothing squirts out!" But nobody listened to him and Hova made that thing make different sounds when he rubbed faster and slower and when he stretched the horse hair tighter and looser and the noise sure was growly like it was rummeling someplace right in your middle and it sure wasn't a country love song but it was almost like something a person might want to sing to Shaftich Shreeda's daughter Fleeda on a hot summer evening.

"Holem de gruel! Where did you get that thing?"

Hova stopped rubbing. "I made it. Grandfather told me how to make it."

"So what's it for?"

"For Sylvesterabend. For New Year's Eve."

"You mean you will play that thing in the church?"

"No, no, you don't play this thing in the church. You go around to people's houses. You get dressed up like on Halloween and go around with the brummtupp and sing a song and do a bit of dummheit."

"You mean shoevanack like on Halloween?"

"No, you just act some dummheit." And then Hova Jake told us about the brummtupp, what his grandfather said, and, I think, some things that only Hova Jake would think of, like he said that the brummtupp was something the Flat Germans used to do on Sylvesterabend because there was no hydro so they couldn't have church in the evening all the time. But now that there is electric light all over the place some think that people should be in the church all the time. "No, I don't think you would play a brummtupp in the church," but it almost seemed to me like Hova's head was working overtime again because all of a sudden he was giving us all orders and we had to practice something that Hova made up as he went along and now I'm on the back of the truck with a dress on. And Penzel Panna has wrapped himself in a red blanket with a floppy red hat on his head and Hova calls him a pope. Hingst is wearing a high fur cap and has a real big bushy mustache so he can be a czar. I don't know where Hova found such a thing but Kunta has on one of those black jackets like the Brunk Tent Crusade preachers have, and Laups has on an army suit and is carrying his air rifle with a rubber knife tied on the end. Hova has on barn clothes, overalls, four-buckles, and one of those leather helmet caps with fur ear flaps.

The truck is slowing down. Kunta Klassen stands up from where he has been huddling under his cow leather blanket.

"We're stopping by Hauns Jaunses' Fraunz."

"Now why are we stopping by Fraunz's place?" Penzel wants to know.

"Because he's home, dummkopp. Most of the people are at church." Hova stops on the road because the driveway is full with snow and for sure all we would need yet is to get the truck stuck. I mean, who could drive a tractor with a dress and lipstick on? Hova leaves the truck running and we sneak to the house. Just a little light comes from one window because Fraunz doesn't have hydro.

Hova carries the brummtupp into the little porch and sets it on the wooden step. We follow. He starts to rub the horse hair. The brummtupp brumms. Hova Jake starts to sing.

Brummtupp Brummtupp
Here comes the Brummtupp
Make open the door
You crazy old boar
And give us some wine
You silly old swine
Or we'll throw your hat
To Sylvester the cat

And all the time Hova is rubbing the horse hair up and down like he is pumping something and that brummtupp is rummeling hartsoft loud and Fraunz opens the door looking like he was sleeping but Hova doesn't wait for him to say nothing, he just pushes the brummtupp through the door in front of him and we go after. In the lamplight of Fraunz's kitchen Laups can see enough through the nylons pulled over his face to poke his stick through the hole in the pig bladder stretched over the night pail and he pushes the stick in and out of the hole, making a higher sound than Hova. They both play away like crazy and I'm thinking it's a good thing that Fraunz doesn't have a dog or we'd be in trouble. Suddenly they stop and it's so quiet you can hear the flames in the tin stove.

"Vowt vell ye met me?" Fraunz asks, taking a step backwards.

"Schmuynge," Kunta says behind me and he pushes me to Fraunz. Fraunz blinkers his eyes like he is a bit scared and I don't know what to do because nobody told me that if I had a dress on I would have to do stuff like a woman, too, and Kunta says again, "Susch wants to schmuynge with you Fraunz. She wants to be you good." And those badels shove me against Fraunz so the windballs in Muttachi's size 49 brassiere press right against him and I am looking over his shoulder counting the flies on the flypaper that is still hanging there from the summer. Then those badels turn my neck so I have to look in Fraunz's eyes and he still looks scared but he seems to be sparkling a little too and Hova Jake shouts, "Give her a kiss!" The brummtupp starts the noise again and Fraunz gets this funny look on his face and I can smell the fried sausage and onions and old sweat and he makes his mouth into a pointed suction cup like they do in the comics and he comes closer and I try to wrench myself away but those badels hold me still and that bristly suction cup gets me right on the lipstick smeared on my mouth. It seems like it will take forever and my windballs are almost pressed flat and I'm wishing they would blow up and blast everybody out of there. I'm getting already mad when suddenly Fraunz jerks away and he holds his fist like he's going to plow me one.

"Fraunz!" Hova shouts. Fraunz freezes. "Vua rum best du nich en ne Choyck? Angst die nich dowt kullde Zoyck?" Fraunz gets white as snow in the face and his fist falls to his side and swings his arm like it was maybe broken. We fly out the door and Hova Jake shouts again, "How come you're not in the church so often? Aren't you afraid of that cold, cold coffin?"

"Susch, Susch, what did you do to poor Fraunz that he got so mad?"

"Yeah, hey what did you do?"

"Nothing!" I say, but somebody did and I don't know who or what and I am mad, only I don't want to show it. I have to laugh a little though when I remember how Fraunz made a suction cup out of his lips, but I figure I'll get even with those badels somehow.

The next place is Zoop Zack Friesen's and he is usually very friendly. Hova rummels the brummtupp at the door and calls, "Portzelcke, Fortzelcke, Shpecka Droats Tien! Sylvester chempt met dei Fortz Machine!"

The door opens and Zoop Zack and his wife and kids are there listening to the radio, country songs, and I wish Hova would stop his brummtupp because I want to hear my best song finish. But he keeps making the fartzing noise. The Friesens are very quiet, listening, the children a little scared and the wife looking us on with pointed eyes trying to see who we are. But we don't say nothing, so she can't figure us out I don't think. Zoop Zack sits by the table drinking out a brown bottle.

The brummtupp stops. Hova Jake makes his voice real low, "Opp en desh doa shteit ne buddel bae'a, Vaae doa von drinkt dei shtinkt!" The children and the wife hurry look to their father and Hova gives the brummtupp one more rubbing fortz and we hurry out because Zoop Zack is rising from his chair. We shout as we run to the truck, "On the table there stands a bottle beer, Who there from drinks he stinks!"

I have almost forgotten about Fraunz's kiss when we stop by Beluira Bergen's and we can see already through the window Mrs. Beluira Bergen with her ear to the phone and her hand over the speaking part. Hova knocks on the door, opens it and leads us in. Mrs. Beluira Bergen lets the phone fall from her hand and Hova and Laups start their brummtupps making hartsoft noise and Beluira Bergen comes running from the back of the house and he has only one morning shoe on and his pants are open and he is pulling his combination underwear over his shoulder. Hova plays louder, then stops sudden and says, "Who picks the phone up when it rings a neighbor's number, her ears will shring!" Mrs. Beluira Bergen gets red in the face and she hurry jumps to put the receiver back on the phone and Beluira is looking from the brummtupp to his wife and the phone, then it looks like he will get mad so Hova says again like he did at Fraunz's, "Vua rum seh ye nich en ne Choyck? Angst yuehnt nicht dowt kullde Zoyck?" Then he gives the brummtupp two terrible rubs and we hurry ourselves outside.

Next at Bulla Buhr's we sing:

Bulla Buhr he had a car
Parley Boo
Bulla Buhr he had a car
Parley Boo
The steer it was from a buggy wheel
The windshield was from onion peel
Hinky Dinky Parley Boo

And Bulla Buhr thinks this is pretty funny and he likes the song until Hova Jake stops playing the brummtupp and says, "Purple gas, purple gas, just in the truck! Purple gas in the car will be bad luck!" Bulla Buhr swears and looks like he will come after us but he stops dead in his tracks when we all say the verse about the cold cold grave and how come he isn't in church.

It's a good thing that in Gutenthal most people go to church so there aren't that many people we can go to visit. Really, now there is left only Willy Wahl. He hardly ever goes to church. But he has an English wife and that bothers some people. And Willy doesn't make her weed beets in summer. That sure bothers some of the men. They think there is something wrong with Willy that he lets his wife, Serena, lie around in the sun with hardly any clothes on. But then Willy was in the army and you sure wouldn't learn nothing good there. I think Serena is pretty nice. One time she had a flat tire close to where I was fixing fence, so I helped her and she was very friendly and not at all scared to get her hands dirty like the women say about her. I figure they probably won't be home. I mean, they could go to a dance in Emerson or something like that.

But the lights are on at Willy Wahl's. When the brummtupp starts up Willy swings the door wide open and welcomes us in.

"Serena! Come look at what has come to wish us a happy New Year!"

Serena hurries into the kitchen from a back room and laughs when she sees us.

"Mummers! How nice! We used to have them when I was a girl in Newfoundland. What a pleasant surprise!" And she comes close to us and looks us over and I am wondering what a mummer is but figure that for sure I must be one because I have a dress on. Serena has a dress on too, dark blue with some shiny silvery stuff in it and it sure fits her good and it looks like they must be getting ready to go some place because Willy has his Sunday suit on. "Willy, you must give them a New Year's drink."

While Willy goes into a back room Hova Jake starts up the brummtupp again, rubbing the horse tail between his fingers, making the stretched cowhide vibrate over the nail barrel and the rummeling noise seems to go right through the barrel, along the floorboards, into the bones and Serena goes closer to Hova, staring at the brummtupp, at Hova's fingers rubbing and stroking the whisk of horse tail, changing the sounds, like a pulse, or a John Deere two-cylinder at different speeds, a sound that seems to come out of the earth. Serena reaches out her hand, touches the stretched cowhide, feels the sound. Laups Leeven gets jealous, so he starts poking his stick through the hole in the pig's bladder stretched over the night pail, but Serena doesn't even notice him. Willy returns with a bottle of wine and Serena gets some cups. The noise stops, we take the cups of wine. I sip it carefully, it tastes kind of sour but it's the first time I ever tasted real wine. Still it seems to go good with the sound of the brummtupp I still feel in my bones.

Serena studies each of us trying to figure out who we are. When she comes to me she tries to see my eyes and I see a funny look like if she is teasing, that she is thinking about some kind of joke, and I look away from her eyes and see the lipstick from my lips on the cup and I sure feel silly, I mean to be dressed up like a woman in front of somebody so beautiful.

"And you're the shortest so they made you put on the dress. It's not quite fair, is it? But you're a good sport. You deserve a reward." And before I know it she is kissing me right on the lips, holding my head between her hands and her tongue pushes in between my teeth and it's like the earth is melting it is such a feeling that I don't even think that her husband, Willy Wahl, is standing right there. And the other guys don't make a sound. They don't play the brummtupp. And when Serena lets me go after about five minutes it sure looks to me like those guys all have their mouths open and their tongues hanging out.

Sure, once we are back on the truck the guys start teasing me, but it doesn't bother me one bit because I know they are jealous. That's right. None of them have ever been kissed by such a hartsoft beautiful woman. I mean, they are lucky if their grandmothers have kissed them. So I'm not even listening to Penzel Panna and Kunta Klassen, just remembering.

"Hey, we're at the church!" Penzel says.

"Yeah, what does Hova want here?"

I get up from my corner of the box. Sure enough we are at the church. The lights are on and the yard is still full with cars. Hova steps out of the cab onto the running board.

"Hey, what are we doing here?"

"Yeah, how come we're at the church?"

"Shh!" Hova says. "We still have to put on the play."

"What play?"

"You know. The one we practiced in the barn."

"You mean in the church?"

"Yeah."

"No way! My folks are in there."

"All of our folks are in there."

"So let's just go home."

"Look, you guys," Hova says. "We're in trouble already because we missed church. Now if you do it my way I don't think anything will happen."

"Oh, yeah. We go in the church with this dummheit and there'll be trouble for sure," Penzel says. "My old man said if I don't behave myself he won't let me get driver's till I'm seventeen!"

"No, no," Hova says. "Just do what we practiced in the barn and everybody will be fine. Just trust me."

I think we are all pretty scared, except Hova Jake, but he is right. We are in trouble already, so what else can go wrong?

Still, I'm all mixed up about what Hova Jake is trying to do. Sure I know what we practiced in the barn but it doesn't make sense to me. We sneak in the back door down into the church cellar and then up the stairs to the door that opens into the church in front beside the steps leading up to the platform. We huddle behind the door and we can hear Preacher Janzen still preaching his Sylvester preach and like always he is using up two times as many words as he needs to say something. Hova Jake presses something cold into my hand. Shit, yeah, I forgot to bring one. Preacher Janzen stops talking. Hova Jake gives the signal. He starts to play the brummtupp. The door opens and I am pushed and then I am standing in front of the church with an apple in my hand. I am very scared so I just do what Hova Jake said to do. I eat the apple. I walk around in front of the church biting and chewing. All of a sudden something hits my arm and the apple goes flying away under the first church bench. Penzel Panna in his red pope suit is standing over me and shaking his long pointing finger and giving me a real dirty look and I try to run from him like Hova said and the red pope grabs me and starts to dance with me. The brummtupp is brumming and I'm trying to fight myself away. Then I see Hingst with his fur hat and czar mustache waving to me and calling me with his finger so I tear away from the pope and run to the czar and he takes me by the hand and starts dancing with me and he goes faster and faster and round and around and then all of a sudden Laups is there with his air rifle and he kills the czar and grabs me and starts to dance holding his air rifle in one hand and we are dancing. Kunta Klassen comes with his Brunk Tent Crusade jacket and he shakes his forefinger, then his fist, and then he reaches his hand out to me and I come away from Laups in his army outfit and go to Kunta who doesn't dance with me. Kunta sits me down on the front church bench instead. Then he waves to the pope and the czar and the soldier and they all come and sit on the church bench. The brummtupp gets louder. Hova Jake marches out with his overalls and four-buckles, his leather helmet cap with fur earflaps. He marches first to the pope and brumms the brummtupp in front of him real loud till the pope gets scared and runs out the back of the church. Then Hova chases the czar away, the soldier, and then the States preacher, till I'm sitting all alone. Hova takes my hand and stands me up and turns me so I'm looking at the church.

The brummtupp plays real quiet, like it's getting the beat ready for a song, and even in the barn when Hova was practicing it didn't sound like that. It still reaches something deep inside the blood but it's not so simple, it's almost like some music I heard on CFAM once with my crystal radio and I couldn't get any other station and then Hova Jake starts to sing:

Joyful, joyful, we adore thee, God of Glory, Lord of Love;
Hearts unfold like flow'rs before Thee, Op'ning to the sun above.

And even though Hova is singing quite quietly there is power in that singing that I don't think anybody ever heard in the Gutenthal church before.

Melt the clouds of sin and sadness, drive the dark of doubt away.
Giver of immortal gladness, fill us with the light of day.

Then Hova starts to give her gas. He sings like he means it. He sings with his whole body. I mean, he really gives her shit! Yeah, his whole body, not just his mouth, no everything, everything that God made him, from his hair to his toes, every little thing is singing this song.

All thy works with joy surround Thee, Earth and heav'n reflect
    Thy ray:
Stars and angels sing around Thee, center of unbroken praise.
Field and forest, vale and mountain, flow'ry meadow,
    flashing sea.
Chanting bird and flowing fountain, call us to rejoice in Thee.

And the people in the church benches are just sitting with their mouths open, wondering over how that badel can sing. Shtemm Gaufel Friesen, the choir leader, can't believe it. Hova never sang like this at choir practice. And even the other guys that got chased away are standing at the door in the back just gawking in wonderment. But Hova hasn't given all yet. He steps on the gas, he opens up the throttle, he is in road gear:

Thou art giving and forgiving, ever blessing, ever blest.
Wellspring of the joy of living, ocean depth of happy rest.
Thou, our Father, Christ our Brother, all who live in love
    are Thine,
Teach us how to love each other, lift us to the joy divine.

And then Hova Jake starts to sing the first verse again and he is signaling the people to stand and slowly they do and they start singing along with him and the sound that is filling the church is just unbelievable. Everybody is singing, even me, and we sing that first verse three times.

"Joyful, joyful we adore Thee, God of Glory, Lord of Love." And we sing it louder each time, but even when I think everybody in the church is singing full blast the brummtupp is still keeping the beat for the song and you can hear it flowing through your bones, through the floor of the church, through the benches, through everybody's bones, up the walls, back and forth, up and down, and it seems almost like the earth and sky are joined or something, I don't know, I can't say for sure, I mean I am there, but well, I just feel all connected up with everything.

Sure, Hova Jake was right. We didn't get into trouble. With such singing how could anybody be mad? And next morning in church who was sitting in the front bench? Hauns Jaunses' Fraunz. Zoop Zack Friesens were in church, too. And Beluira Bergens and Bulla Buhr. Then going the church out at the end I saw Willy Wahl and Serena, and I was bothered. Then it wasn't funny no more. I mean, I really didn't want to see Serena there. I wanted to keep her separate, something special. And I was really mixed up. Everything was connected loose again.

Chapter Three

So goes it then always. Muttachi hears cawing while she milks the schemmel cow with the barn door open and she hurries to the house so fast that the froth from the milk spreads all over the hem of her Robin Hood sack-dress and she runs into the house, cowshit, four-buckles and everything, grabs the flyclapper from the nail by the Booker stove, charges up the stairs to my place under the rafters and smacks me with the flyclapper, the homemade one, made from a hockey stick handle and a piece of old threshing machine belt.

"Yasch, Yasch, stand once already up! The crows are here. Soon is it saddle time. You must find a place to work out for the summer."

Muttachi stops beating the feathers out of the quilt for a second and pulls it off me and starts on my Stanfields, finding quickly the trap door with no buttons.

"Yasch, Yasch, get your narsch out from the bed!"

The trap door is wide open now and my hams begin to smoke, so I throw the pillow off my head, turn quickly over and sit up. I get another smack on my hip.

"Muttachi! What is with you? The milk is getting sour and you bring manure all over the floor. Is you the bearings loose?"

Muttachi lands a good slap on the side of my face and tramps down the stairs. I look slowly out between the Purity flour curtains. Saddle time? Not for a month yet, there's still snow on the ground. Even Haustig Neefeld, who seeds always early enough so his Durum wheat can catch a good snowfall after it's up, won't be out on his field for anyways three weeks.

I lie again down and listen to Muttachi begin turning the crank on the cream separator, hear it speed up, then the hishing sound as she opens the tap to let out the milk from the bowl at the top, then the planging on the bottom of the pails as the milk and the cream run out of the two long spouts.

"Yasch!" she yells over the hum of the separator. "I maybe phone Nobah Naze Needarp to see if he help needs this year again!"

"But not Nobah Naze!" I groan to myself. I worked for him last year and he sure knows how to nutz you out. Up at five o'clock in the morning, cleaning out his barns, hardly nothing to eat, porridge sometimes three meals a day, and work till nine at night. Then he took five bucks off my pay because I got stuck on the field and he had to borrow Zamp Pickle Peters's 4010 to pull me out. And then bringing in bales with his fat daughter who is looking for something she won't get from me. She sticks me in the hind end with a pitchfork handle, and I almost break my neck on the hayrack because Nobah Naze lets out the clutch with a jerk just then and I swear at the cluck and the old man hears it and he tells me to behave with his daughter. No way I'll work for him again.

Then I think about who else Muttachi can phone. We just have farmer phone at our place, so we only can phone to others that have farmer phone, too. Farmer phone is real old phone connected along the fences and about a dozen farmers have it. It doesn't cost nothing, except maybe new batteries sometimes. So Muttachi could phone Hauns Jaunses' Fraunz, but he only has forty acres and his wild oats and fat hen seed themselves. Then there's Schlax Wiebe, the himmelshtenda, you know, about seven feet high, but he has twelve kids so he doesn't need any help. It's his Mumchi that help needs. Muttachi said the Mumchi didn't want to come home from the hospital after the last one. She should hire Schneeda Giesbrecht, the steermaker.

Anyways, I hear the cream separator stop and I figure I'd better hurry downstairs so that I can stop Muttachi from phoning. But when I get downstairs in my felt burr socks, Muttachi is sitting on the bench by the stove holding her back.

"What is loose with you?" I ask and I see she still has the four-buckles on.

"My back is to nothing again. We must to the rightmaker go. Can you let loose the truck?"

"It hasn't been let loose all winter, but I'll see!" I turn to go outside.

"First, help me to go to the beckhouse." Muttachi hangs her arm around my shoulder and I help her outside to the beckhouse there between the washline and the sugar trees. When I have her seated on the left hole, she says, "Oh, thousand, I have the *Steinbach Post* forgotten. Please it to me bring. Leave open the door. Then I can see who goes by."

After I bring her the German paper I go over to the old Chevy truck. It's a good truck from spring till fall but as soon as it gets zero degrees cold it won't start. But today I'm lucky, it right away turns over and soon the five cylinders are purring away with hardly a knock. Then it falls me by that I didn't buy licence for this year yet, so I creep out of the truck and look at the plates. They are yellow, just like the new ones, so I take a couple of handfuls of mud and smatter it over the licence so that you can't see what year it is from.

Then I go back to the beckhouse, thinking Muttachi must have got frostbite on her thresher loaves already, but she is rubbing her nose over the *Steinbach Post* finding out all about our third and fourth cousins in Paraguay.

After I get Muttachi loaded onto the piece of plyboard which lies on the woman's side of the seat so the springs can't poke, I quickly check to see that the tires are full of wind. One of the Knobbies in the back is a little soft so I figure we'll have to stop at the store for some free air.

Store Janzen's Willy is busy filling Ha Ha Nickel's Buick up with gas when I stop by the free air hose. Ha Ha's daughter Sadie (only fifteen but Ha Ha lets her drive already the car) is leaning against the side of the Buick in her curling sweater and tight ski pants making me wish I was sixteen instead of twenty-three and that I could work for Ha Ha Nickel. But Sadie drives the tractors, too, and so I don't think Ha Ha will need any help.

Anyway, Willy finishes filling the tank and Sadie tells him to write it on the bill. Then she spins her tires in the slush and streaks off down the road. I think maybe I should fill some gas up too but Janzen won't let me write it on any more so I have to wait to see if I'll get another Unemployment cheque. When the Knobby is full of wind again Muttachi and I set off down the Post Road to Knibble Thiessen's place close to town.

Knibble Thiessen is what we Flat Germans call a gooseberry boor. That means he isn't a farmer, but lives on a farmyard with a bit of livestock and a small garden, maybe even a gooseberry bush or two, and makes ends meet with odd jobs and little sidelines like saw sharpening and firewood cutting. Knibble Thiessen his father's fingers has and is like his father was, a rightmaker, or bone setter, so he doesn't do so much at all in the way of farming or other footlicking jobs. Not now in the last few years since the women from the States have found out about him.

Mind you, bone setting is pretty good business around here. A person could find half-a-dozen and use up only a dollar's worth of gas, but most can't make a complete living from it. Many of the rightmakers are old folks, on pension already, who knibble because their fathers knibbled and the people keep coming even after the old people have gone dead.

You see, people go to the knibbler because a rightmaker isn't a high person like a doctor. A doctor is learned so high that people are scared and you have to talk English—sometimes to a Catholic yet! Even the Flat German ones have often learned themselves away from the *schmallen Lebensweg*—even so far as the United Church!

And then doctors don't always know for sure what is loose with you anyway and you could almost go dead while they try this pill and that needle. But with a rightmaker it's like visiting neighbors and he always knows what is loose and he makes it right and for a dollar you are not to nothing any more.

You learn this from young on. If your thumb gets ducked out by a baseball at school, you just go to the rightmaker in the evening and sit down in the big room with the other people and look around at the Sunday dishes in the glass cupboards and smell the strange liniments coming from behind the curtain that leads to the little room. Soon you hear a chair drag on the floor, then underskirts whispering, or some suspenders clapping into place. Apart moves the curtain and the fixed-up one comes out and you can go in with your thumb. Maybe it does a little bit hurt when the old man pulls on the thumb, then wiggles and twists and slips the joint into the right place. But then it is fixed up good.

Now Knibble Thiessen's place is different from these older places. He has a *clinic* apart from the house, maybe because his wife is tired with having all the time strangers under the feet, or maybe she likes not to be so close to where her man is knibbling these women from the States with their red lips and earrings. Yes, Thiessen is getting to be a real spitz poop. His sign doesn't say 'Bone Setter'; it says 'Knockenartzt' in German letters, and then 'General Massage.' He has office hours regular and even old magazines to read in the waiting room. I think he gets them from his barber cousin in Winkler after nobody wants to read them there any more.

Muttachi has been reading the *Steinbach Post* ever since we left home, never saying a word, not even about the naked woman air freshener that hangs from the mirror, but now she bends the paper in two and says, "Something new again. It says in the *Post* that Knibble Thiessen has just come from California back where he learned about feet rubbing. With feet rubbing it says he can fix anything that is to nothing."

Sure enough, when I drive in by Knibble Thiessen's he has a new sign up, 'Foot Masseur,' and the yard is full of vehicles with black and white licenses.

"Huy Yuy Yuy," says Muttachi. "This will long take. It's good I only half finished the *Steinbach Post*." I help Muttachi down and lead her to the door.

Inside it is full, all women, States women with red lips and earrings, some so small they look like warts, others so big you can't see the ear at all. There is only one place to sit, the end of an old church bench that Thiessen got when he ripped down an old church in the days when knibbling only an evening job was. Carefully, I help Muttachi sit half of her hind quarter next to a black-haired, tall woman with a fur jacket over her black dress. Her lips and fingernails are red like Shuzzel Shroeder's new pig barn and she is smoking with a long thin holder a cigarette. She lays one long thin leg over the other when Muttachi sits down and the hem of her black skirt pulls up over her knee a little and shows the shiny black underskirt.

The woman doesn't pull down her skirt, but she moves her fishnet stocking leg away so that her ankle-high pointed overshoe won't touch Muttachi's four-buckles. Muttachi has already opened her *Steinbach Post* again and I see that two-thirds of her seat is on the bench now and I know that she will be quite soon comfortable.

Since all the seats are taken I kneel down beside Muttachi and reach for the heap of magazines on the little table that I saw at Winkle Wieler's outcall sale. Everybody went to that sale because the outcallers were the Flying Hieberts, the Singing Auctioneers, who always start the outcall with singing the auctioneer song.

I am looking through the *Young Ambassadors* and *Good News Broadcasters* to find a *Time* magazine when the door from the inner room opens and a girl with a cowboy hat comes out. She has on a white shirt with a tight black vest and her black pants are so snug that Muttachi goes, "Huy Yuy Yuy!" The girl's waist is so thin against the other parts of her that I think I could reach around her with one hand. But all this is nothing like the look on her face. It is pure Himmel-shine, like the look I once saw when I was a little bengel boy visiting some neighbors and they had this calendar with a picture of a cowgirl who had such a look on her face and under the picture were words from the song, "I'll be a cowgirl, a Christian cowgirl."

Then Knibble Thiessen steps out beside her, in his hands some red cowboy boots. Only then do I see her bare feet, feet that seem to sparkle and glow like Jesus's feet did when Mary washed them with her hair, and it is a shame that those feet have to touch the waiting room floor that is all tracked with mud. The girl takes the boots from Knibble but she doesn't put them on. Instead, she walks over the muddy floor, opens the door and steps on the icy stoop. The cold shakes her out of her dream and she steps quickly back inside, wipes her feet with her hand and pulls the boots on. Then she laughs as she quickly glances the room around and hops the door out.

Knibble Thiessen flashes a quick smile around the room and I notice that he has grown a beard to hide the place where he should have a chin and he is wearing oil in his hair. His smile sours a bit when he sees me and Muttachi, but it quickly shines up when he asks, "Who is next?" and the thin woman beside

Muttachi rises up from her seat so eagerly that she rubs her leg against Muttachi's four-buckles and a little white line starts running up the fishnet. But the woman doesn't even notice as she runs into the back room.

Knibble hurries the door closed after himself and the waiting women make eyes with each other, then look back into their magazines. Muttachi has slid over on the bench so that she is as close to the next woman as she was to the fishnet lady and she waves me to sit beside her. The red-haired woman with green eyelids gives me a dirty look when I sit down. Then she stretches out her legs that are inside green pants, the kind that are stretchy and have to have a strap that goes under the foot like hockey socks. I once wanted a pair of hockey socks like that but Muttachi wouldn't let me buy some. Instead, she knitted me some that she said would keep my feet warm, too. Only she didn't enough red wool have for the second one so she finished it with purple and yellow. Muttachi wouldn't let me buy some hockey garters either, but made me some from a pink girdle that Futtachi gave her for Christmas before he took the trip to Mexico to visit his uncle and never came back. Word came back to Muttachi that Futtachi had last been seen driving through the village with his arm around a Spanish girl. Then he was found with a knife in his back at the bottom of a cliff. Muttachi doesn't believe a word of it and she still hopes that he will come back.

All of a sudden comes a soft cry from the back room. Muttachi stops in the middle of paging the *Post*. The woman closest to the door is just lighting a cigarette and she holds the burning match an inch away from the end. We all listen. The cry comes again, slowly growing into a shriek. The match burns the lady's finger and she whispers, "Shit," and we all let out our breath again as she lights another match.

Again starts the cry, louder and louder till it is such a katzen-jammer I wonder if it will the windows break. Then there are moans that go up and down, soft and loud and I can't say for sure if it's because something hurts or because something feels good and I think of the time Hingst Heinrichs's Futtachi wrote me out a beet-weeding cheque and on the bottom he writes 'For Labor' and I remember Schacht Schulz, who was holding school then, made us write it 'Labour' so I say to Heinrichs, "Shouldn't it be 'o-u-r'?" and he says, "Only if it hurts." Schacht Schulz didn't like that when I said it to him.

Everything is quiet. Then the door opens and the fishnet lady comes out—in her stocking feet, a big smile on her mouth, but a tear leaking through the red patch on her cheek. Knibble slips behind her and holds up her pointy-toed overshoes. The fishnet lady gets red and says, "Oh, thank you!" and she takes them slowly from him, then holds herself steady on his elbow as she slides each fishnet foot into the overshoes and her toes wiggle inside like tadpoles in a pail of ditch water.

She steps frontwards, wobbles a little on the spike heels, and walks to the door. The red-haired woman with the green eyelids gets quickly up and hurries into the back room before Knibble can ask who next is.

The two doors close behind the two women at the same time and the woman who got her cigarette lit at last blows a big smoke ring into the middle of the room. I watch the ring get bigger as it floats over the little table, then starts to curl like Ball Bearing Bertha's hula hoop did in the baseball team's weiner roasting fire, the year we beat the Morden Farmers at the Sports Day, the same night that Zoop Zack Friesen saw the UFO land on the roof of his new machine shed and now he goes to the free church three times a week and won't play with us baseball any more.

Outside a car motor lets loose and right away the engine revs full throttle and I hear singing rubber so I jump up to the door and see the fishnet lady spinning her white Chrysler tires. The air stinks from hot rubber when I get outside. So I holler at her and wave my arms and she sees me and takes her foot off the gas and the tires stop in three-inch holes that fit perfect.

I walk up to the car and the back window on the other side slides down, then the front one goes half-way and stops. I see her hand jerk and the two windows on the driver's side come down together and I lean my elbows on the bottom of the window and look in. The woman turns her face red to me and I can see the layers of black below her white neck under the fur of the coat and I say, "We can try to rock it out."

So I bring it by to her what I mean and I go to the back of the car and get ready to lift when she starts to drive again. I grab the bumper and lift when she steps on the accelerator, then she lets it up and steps on it again and each time she steps on it I lift up with all my might and slowly the car starts to rock, back and forth as I bend up and down and the fishnet lady pushes the footfeed in and out and the car bounces higher and higher and I give one humdinger of a lift and the car hops out from the holes and pain shoots up my back and the fishnet lady's tires spray snow all over me as I sink to the frozen ground.

The Chrysler swerves on to the road and the lady never looks back to see me sprawled on the packed snow beside the black holes smelling with hot rubber. The cold seepers through my clothes as I lie so that it doesn't hurt so much and I hear a crow caw somewhere to the left of my head, then another one to the right and I think that if Muttachi hadn't heard the crow this morning I wouldn't be lying here listening to some more crows, while my shanks are getting numb.

"Corbies," I mutter. "Twa Corbies!" Like the verse Schacht Schulz made us learn off by heart that time me and Yodelling Abe Wiebe played hookey and every day for two weeks he made us stand up and say it before he let us go home. 'As I was walking all alane I herd twa corbies making a mane. The tane unto t' other say Where sall we gang and dine today.'

"Yasch, Yasch, what is loose with you now?" I turn, starting the pain again, and see Muttachi come down the steps

40

in her brown woman's stockings, holding her four-buckles in her left hand.

"My back is to nothing!" I whine, and Muttachi stops in her tracks, turns and hobbles back into the clinic. A moment later she drags Knibble Thiessen across the yard. Knibble kneels down and is going to help me up but Muttachi has already my boots pulled off.

"Here, fix him up like you me fixed!"

So Knibble my bluing feet attacks, pinching and rubbing, making me hurt all over my body, not just my back. He makes the pain jump from my leg to my shoulder to my narsch to my belly and then between the legs and I start to twitch around in the snow and I think I will go crazy until Knibble stops and says, "Stand up."

Sure enough, the pain is away and I get on my feet up and hurry into my boots. "See Yasch, with feet rubbing he can fix anything that is to nothing. Now we can find you a place to work out."

Knibble understands quickly what Muttachi means and he sees there is a way that he might some day from us get paid, so he says, "Yeah, Ha Ha Nickel's Mumchi was here yesterday to get her feet rubbed and she said Ha Ha wants to hire a man this year."

"See, with feet rubbing he can fix up everything," Muttachi laughs. "Come, Yasch, we hook on by Ha Ha Nickel before we go home."

Chapter Four

I like to work for Ha Ha Nickel. When you work for Ha Ha you don't have to string yourself on for everything like by Nobah Naze Needarp. No sir, with Ha Ha not everything has to be done by wrenching around with the back, so I don't feel all used up at fire evening.

Last year I had to stop pitching for the ball team because Nobah Naze wouldn't lower himself to borrow Hingst Heinrichs's Ford with the post hole digger because Heinrichs's father-in-law had once opened a culvert and flooded Nobah Naze's father's field. So I had to dig a hundred holes by hand and my pitching arm got all to nothing, so that even after Knibble Thiessen, the rightmaker, fixed it I could only give three of my windmill upshoot drop curves before I was all used up.

And then Oata Needarp, Nobah Naze's two-hundred-pound daughter, always wanted along to the ball game, which was bad enough. Only Nobah Naze didn't want Oata to go. He said she should stay home and practice her correspondence piano lessons so she someday in the church could play. Well, Oata couldn't hold a tune if it was made of flypaper, and she knew it, too! I mean, Schacht Schulz used to tell her not to sing at the Christmas program and if anybody could make a person to sing *he* could.

Anyways, the first ball game I had to make fire evening early for Oata asks me if her I will take along. Nobah Naze says, "No, you must home stay to fix the house ready for when Mama comes on Sunday." Nobah Naze's Mumchi stays in a hospital for people not all correct in their heads and only comes home to visit once in a month, but my Muttachi said me one time that Nobah Naze was so afraid that she would look on another man that he kept her always at home and wouldn't her even to church take.

Well, it didn't make me no never mind that Oata couldn't go along because it laughered the ball team enough already that I was working by Nobah Naze, leave alone hauling the fat cluck around.

So I drove away in my old Chevy half-ton, thinking I would have had to put more wind in the tires on the woman's side if Oata had come along. About a mile and a half down the road something started to hammer on my back window and sure as a stone is hard there was Oata standing in the box of my truck.

I wondered what would laugher the team more: Oata in the box or Oata on the piece of plyboard on the woman's side of the seat. I couldn't see much choice of freedom there at all so I held the truck still.

Before the wheels stopped quite rolling Oata helped herself up on to the roof of the cab and I heard the tin buckling over my head. Then the windshield got dark as Oata's half-section of hinterland slid down the dividing post to the hood. Lucky, my truck is made from old Coca Cola signs instead of tobacco cans like the new ones are.

Oata slid off from the hood to the fender and crept into the cab, onto the plyboard. The springs twanged as I glutzed at her. Her one brown eye and one blue eye glutzed right back at me and she said, "Well, zippa your fly shut an' let's go!"

I jerked down my eyes, then I floored the footfeed and popped the clutch. The truck stayed still.

"Hey, Penzel, you should shift the gear in!"

"Dievel, Deivel, Dunna, and Schinda! Mustard Boar!"

"Na, na, Penzel, such big words you know," she said, and then she called me Penzel for the whole summer.

No, sir, with Ha Ha Nickel such troubles I don't have. It's like antonyms the difference. Take like Sadie Nickel. If Oata is a half-section, Sadie is one track of the field road. Yes sir, Sadie is like a forked willow stick, up side down. Skin and bones, yes, but such skin, tanned nice brown, not sour creamfat white like Oata's. And bones, bones that move when she walks. "Dem dry bones," I sing all day on the tractor. "Dry bones, I hear de word of de Lord," like the Blackwood Brothers on that old wind-up gramophone.

And can she catch a baseball! Everyday after fire evening she backs up against the machine shop door and I practice my pitching with her. She hardly never misses even when sometimes my windmills go wild. She bends and stretches so easy, so lightly she hops up for the high ones. And so we play catch till her mother calls her in to do her homework so she can pass her grade ten at the collegiate institute in town.

Me, I took grade ten with correspondence the year after Schacht Schulz had learned himself high enough to teach in an English town so we had a permit teacher who had enough trouble trying to learn Pug Peters to write his name, leave alone learn me algebra. Everything else I passed, but algebra not.

Anyway, one evening after I wash my truck and it's quite dark already and Ha Ha and his wife have gone visiting I go into the house. I start to go down into the basement where my room is and Sadie calls, "Yasch, can you help me with this?"

I go up into the kitchen where Sadie is sitting with a towel around her head and wearing one of those housecoats made from stuff like towel only softer.

"What can I do you for?" I say, trying not to look too hard at those bony knees poking out past the end of the white cloth.

"Did you ever do sight poems when you went to school?"

"What kind of poems?" I lean closer to see what kind of papers she has in front of her.

"Sight poems," she says. "You know, the teacher gives you a poem with some questions and you have to read the poem and answer them."

"Oh yeah, I think so, maybe."

"Here, look at this. It doesn't make any sense. It's like French or something."

I take the paper with the purple typing on it and start to laugh. "'Twa Corbies.' Ha Ha Ha. You know Schacht Schulz made me and Yodelling Abe Wiebe learn this off by heart once when we had played hookey. 'As I was walking all alane I herd twa corbies making a mane.'"

I look down at Sadie and her dark brown eyes shine up at me.

"Then you know what it means?"

"Oh sure," I say and I look at Sadie's brown neck reaching up into the white towel cloth. She reaches up her arms and pulls the towel off and the clean smell from her washed hair comes into my nose. I start to smell myself. The salty rings under my arms.

"Well, tell me what it means." She takes a comb from the table and starts to untangle her damp hair.

"Well," I say, and I sit down on a chair, holding the sheet out with one hand, putting the other hand up to my chin to feel the three-day-old beard. "You see, this poem is like it was made up from Flat German mixed up with English. Except for corbies. Corbies are crows. That's what Schacht Schulz's book said. You see, his book had notes that said what everything means.

And then Schacht Schulz always tried to bring things by to us, even if we didn't want to know."

"You mean the poem is about crows?"

"Yeah, two crows. Twa corbies. As I was walking all alane. Alane is like *allein* in German. I herd two corbies making a mane. Mane could be like a horse's mane or it could be the Main Street. Anyways, the crows are making a mane. The tane unto t' other say. The tane, that's the one with the big tooth, and he says to the other one, Where sall we gang and dine today? Sall is like zell in Flat German and gang is like gang in German, only it means not the place between the house and the barn like they have in the old darps. See these crows can talk and one asks the other one where they shall eat today."

And so I try to bring it by to her that the verse is all about how these crows plan to eat this dead guy that is lying behind this old full ditch, only nobody knows about him except the guy's hawk, his dog, and his girlfriend who has run off with another guy.

Sadie leans back as she listens to me and I almost lose the string of the story when she puts her feet up on the table. I quickly hold the paper in front of my face so that my eyes don't bounce out on to her bones under that gold brown skin. I have come to the part about the guy's banes and I make her to understand that there are two kinds of banes. The white hause-bane is the upstairs of his house and that the other banes are bones. The wind is going to blaw like a cow blaws over the bones for evermair. I stare at those long clean toes on the table and a little wind comes through the window screen and I see tiny little hairs wiggle on the sunburned leg. The grime between my toes starts to crawl.

"That's all it's about?" Sadie sounds a little disappointed.

"Yeah, that's about it." I want to say more but I'm suddenly very uncomfortable with her, so I give her the sheet back and hurry down into the basement. I feel terribly dirty and I decide to try out the new showerbath Ha Ha has put into the basement.

It feels good to stand in the rain of the showerbath and have the summerfallow wash off into the drain and I even let myself think about how Sadie must have stood here, too, only a little while ago, but I get a little nervous and my head starts to reach back to Futtachi, my father.

Futtachi went down to Mexico to visit his uncle and never came back. Muttachi didn't go with because she gets sick when she rides in the car too long. Anyway, we haven't heard from Futtachi since then. Muttachi thinks he will come back, but I know better now. I found it out from a Flat German Mexican last year when the ball team went to the beer parlor in Neche. This come back again burro sits down at my table and soon I find out that he comes from my uncle's darp down there. The other guys at the table are busy watching the muskmelons shaking in the waitress's blouse, so I quietly ask this Mex if he knows what happened to Futtachi.

So he tells me that his darp was real old-fashioned and that they thought riding in cars was sinful and so nobody would ride in Futtachi's car with him. So one afternoon Futtachi got mad and drove off into the Spanish town and picked up a Spanish girl then drove through the darp honking. Two days later they found Futtachi at the bottom of a cliff with a knife in his back. Nobody in the darp would let on that they knew anything about Futtachi and his wallet and car were gone, so that's why we never heard anything.

The "Twa Corbies" poem made me think of Futtachi and I wish I could tell Sadie about it but at the same time I feel terribly nervous, too.

A few days later is is Himmelfahrt, that Thursday in the spring when Jesus goes to heaven and the Flat Germans go to Winnipeg, if the crop is in. Some people go to church still and the kids are home from school.

Sadie is home from school, too, and Ha Ha has put her to work on the 4010 with the deep tiller on the sixty acres next to

48

the oats that I am seeding. I look over at her as often as I can and I hum "Dry Bones" but Ha Ha Nickel is a plowing match champion and you can never see a wiggle in any of his field work, so I keep my eyes on the mark most of the time, because every move you make when pulling a drill shows when the grain comes up. And then everybody can laugh at your wiggly rows.

And for sure I don't want Sadie to laugher herself over my field. Not now that I shave myself every day and even smear on some green shaving lotion from the Rawleigh man.

Ha Ha picks us up for dinner and I creep into the truck after Sadie and I see the black straps shining through her white shirt. Ha Ha speeds around the correction line in the dirt road and Sadie's hip bone digs into my shank and when her hand grabs my leg when we dip through the spillway at the dike I am happy for sure that my shirt is only from yesterday clean.

After dinner Sadie has on old blue jeans that are ripped off over the knees and I have to look very steady at the spider web crack in the windshield. We let Sadie off at the 4010 and go to the drill and I start to fill the seeder box up while Ha Ha checks up the fertilizer. I look to the next field and I have to hold myself on the seeder box lid. Sadie is on the tractor and she has her shirt taken off and has on just a black brassiere.

"Look out for the crows, Yasch," Ha Ha laughs and he slams down the fertilizer lid.

"Twa corbies," I say, louder than I mean.

"What you say, Yasch?"

"Twa corbies. That's French for two crows."

"I didn't know you was a france hose," Ha Ha laughs. Sadie starts her tractor and I watch as she turns the outfit around and sinks the cultivator shovels deep into the earth. Only the thin black strips that hold up the crows can I see now against the bones of her shoulders.

I wonder myself a little bit how come Ha Ha would such a thing say his own daughter about, but I mean Ha Ha likes to make a joke sometimes. It seems like almost that Ha Ha Nickel isn't scared about such things. It is easy to laugh when you're not scared. But it sure is hard to seed straight when there are crows on the field!

So it goes then good, this working out by Ha Ha Nickel. It is even starting to fall me by why Ha Ha is a good farmer and Nobah Naze isn't. You see, Ha Ha reckons everything out before he does a thing. Then he can always do a thing correct the first time. He always has everything ready what he needs to do a job. By Ha Ha there is never no running forth and back for a crescent, or a cowfoot, or a grease gun because it didn't fall him by.

Now by Nobah Naze Needarp it was enough to make a person to go dizzy always running back for that tool or this pail. One time when I was fencing with him he drove all over his farm for two hours looking for the cowfoot so I could stamp the earth down around the posts. He even told Oata to phone the RCMP that the cowfoot was stolen and it sure was a good thing that she never does what her Futtachi says because she would never have been able to bring it by to the mounties that a cowfoot was a crowbar and had to do nothing with cows or crows or even corbies. When at the end he brought the new shaft he had bought to fix the swather up with, the cowfoot was sticking out from the rumpled tarp in the box of the truck. Nobah Naze got lipstick red like Sawatsky's new barn and he leaned himself on a post and huffed and puffed.

I'm sure glad I'm away from there. Here by Ha Ha Nickel I *like* to work. Muttachi will never believe it, but it's true. I get up in the morning before Ha Ha even has to call down into the basement and I like to go out in the cool air and check the oil on the 4010 and fill some diesel into the tank, and then go to breakfast where Sadie is getting together her books to go to school on the yellow bus with the stop sign on the side.

And I sure sing a lot on the tractor. "Dry Bones" and "You're the nearest thing to heaven, yes you are," which Muttachi gave me the record for once because she thought it was a religious song and would make me want to go to church. Sometimes I even say up "Twa Corbies" all through but that makes me remind about Futtachi and I get chicken skin all over me even if it eighty above is.

So I quickly start to reckon about this plan that I have in my head. I figure if I really work hard and I do a good job and I get Sadie and Ha Ha on my side then just maybe Ha Ha can help me get a start. Maybe I can rent some land, say eighty acres or something, and Ha Ha could sign for me at the Credit Union and borrow me his tractor and disker and things and maybe I could be a farmer and when Sadie is old enough.... Maybe there is a way for someone like me, born on the wrong side of the double dike, to shovel the manure out of my own gutter instead of someone else's.

Sometimes Sadie to the ball games comes along. Then I can always pitch good. I zing 'em in there one two three and next batter up. And when the game is over I don't go with to drink beer down by the big ditch that cuts the United States off from us. Some of the younger ones don't like it that I won't haul out a case for them at the parlor any more, but I for sure don't want my name in the court page in the *Echo* now. Not when Sadie is riding with me.

Sadie sits on the blanket I have put on the plyboard and we don't say much as I drive slowly home. The radio pulls in Portage loud and clear and we listen to the Plains City Roundup and I wonder maybe Sadie would like it if she got a dedication song requested for her, so I ask her what is her favorite song, and she says "Town Without Pity" and I know it is not a western song and they won't play it on the Roundup so it's no use sending in a letter. So I turn the button on the radio till I get to CKY and hope they will play her song. I don't like the rock and roll so much but when I see Sadie's knee bouncing a little I like it better.

51

Just before we get to Ha Ha's long driveway, it is dark enough for the moon to shine and all of a sudden the song comes on and I try to drive very slowly, but it is quite a long song and when we get already to the yard and the song isn't finished I leave the truck running and we listen till the end.

On Sunday Sadie goes to Panzenfeld with me where our team plays against the Fehr brothers. That is so! Every last one of them comes from the same nest and can they all play ball. The youngest is only fourteen in right field, but he can judge a fly ball into his glove with the sun in his eyes. I leave Sadie behind the backstop and say I'll win the game for her.

Winning the Fehrs isn't so easy though. With my pitching I can make it so they can't hit, but they are in the field so good that even with some good hits we can never get farther than first base. So when it's our last time to bat the score is nothing to nothing.

The first two guys get out on pop-ups and then Shuzzel Schroeder is up. Everything gets still when he steps to the base. Then the Fehrs laugher themselves when they see his bat. It is a homemade one turned off on a lathe from a fence pole and you can still the holes in it see from the nails. Shuzzel gives it a few practice swings and then comes the pitch. Shuzzel's bat knacks that ball one and it flies up up up and away so high that we hardly see it and then it comes down real fast and lands on the other side of the fence in a fresh cowpie. The fourteen-year-old Fehr is fast but Shuzzel is over already home plate when the brown ball from the sky comes zinging in.

Our team cheers and claps Shuzzel on the back and I think already to stop by the Dairy Dell with Sadie for a soft ice cream when I feel a poke in the back. It is Sadie and she says she won't ride with me home because she will go to the "Town Without Pity" show in Neche with Pug Peters. I don't even have time to let my tongue loose and she is away.

But I still have to pitch one inning. The back catcher's glove is Pug Peters's head and I burn the balls over the base so that Gopher Goosen has to take off his glove to rub his hand. But nine like that are enough.

It is almost midnight when I am driving back to Ha Ha's from Buffalo Creek where Gopher Goosen had a twenty-four hidden under the bridge. I see some tail lights stop by Ha Ha's driveway then tear off down the road. When I get there Sadie is walking to the yard. I stop and open the door. Sadie creeps into the cab and I smell right away Pug Peters's cigar smoke in her hair. Sadie says nothing. It feels a little bit like I'm a big brother driving his sister home.

The house is all dark. Sadie hops out of the truck and I watch her run to the house. The truck radio plays a Johnny Horton song, "All for the love of a girl," and I sit there feeling the song and wishing that the singer wasn't dead in a car crash and could sing more songs like that. When I go in I hear some footsteps, then a door close someplace. It feels like somebody was watching me.

The next morning Sadie doesn't come for breakfast and Ha Ha says that Nobah Naze Needarp a heart attack has had. He is in the hospital and his crop isn't yet seeded. Ha Ha and some farmers are going over there to see what they can do to help. Ha Ha starts to stand up from the table then he looks me on and says, "Pretty long ball game yesterday." It seems like he will say more, then he puts his John Deere cap on tilted and goes outside.

At dinner time he tells me to take the 4010 and the disker over to Nobah Naze's farm. He figures there is a good week's work to do there.

So I take the machinery over to Needarp's and I am thankful that Ha Ha has parked already the truckful of seed by the field and I don't have to stop to see Oata by the yard. Ha Ha pulls up a few minutes later and he whistles while we fill the seeder box. He doesn't say nothing. He just whistles.

Then I am alone on the field and I try not to think where I am. I just keep my eye on the furrow and try not to feel the poke in my back that I got from Sadie. Half a dozen rounds in the hot sun and I start to get thirsty, but when I reach down beside the seat the water jug isn't there.

All at once I hear a horn off to the side. I turn to look. There is Oata on the Ford tractor, bouncing the field road along, her shirt flying back with the wind. I shove the lever to full throttle, too fast for good seeding, but she keeps getting closer. Then she is even with me and she turns on to the field over the seeded rounds. My dry bones start to rattle and I try to look away but it is like a magnet is pulling my neck around and I feel the wheels hop out of the furrow and I know the seeds are falling in wiggly lines but I just have to try to get away from those two bouncing crows that grow bigger and bigger and bigger!

Chapter Five

With Oata Needarp you never know what she will do. I found that out last year. Working by Nobah Naze was like trying to shovel water with a fork. Nothing would ever work right and then Nobah Naze would always think everything was my fault.

But it was Oata, fat fat Oata that made the summer the worst in my life. I mean, think about this. Two hundred pounds lard chasing me with a pitchfork on the hayfield when Nobah Naze wasn't looking. Or telling Nobah Naze that *I* gave her the pocket book to read with the blouse coming off the shoulders from the woman on the cover. And then Nobah Naze reading me at breakfast from his devotions book about fornification and stuff like that. How was I supposed to help it if Oata didn't want to read Danny Orlis books no more? All the summer through Oata was after me to take her to ball games and Sunday Night Christian Endeavors and if I tried not to take her along she would do something like letting air out of my tires so that by the time I had them full of wind again she would be sitting in the cab waiting. If I tried to sneak away she would have hidden my glove. So she would come along but she wouldn't just be quiet and watch the game like a girl should. She would cheer away like crazy all the time and at one game somebody wrote 'Oata Oata' with lipstick all over the window on my half-ton truck, and I think she did it herself. When the game over was Oata would sit in the truck and honk the horn so I couldn't even neighbor with the other ball players a little bit yet. The few times when I did sneak away from her she poured water or sand in my bed so that I stopped staying there for night and went home to Muttachi's place even if Muttachi was mad with me because she said that Nobah Naze was supposed to give me board *and* room with the job.

It sure didn't put any jam on my bread this morning when Ha Ha sent me to work by Nobah Naze Needarp's because the old man a heart attack had. Now you tell me if it fair is. I mean if Ha Ha Nickel wants to be such a neighborly with-helper all of a sudden, why doesn't he do it himself? For sure it's easy to help out when all he has to do is tell the oabeida to do it. Then it doesn't cost him very much. He doesn't even have to get close to the person that help needs. He doesn't have to feel nothing or deal with nobody. And he gets stars on his crown real easy.

But what about me, the oabeida, the knecht, the hired man? How do you think it feels to be chased across the field by a two-hundred-pound cluck on a Ford tractor? With her blouse open and blowing back in the wind. Is Ha Ha Nickel sitting here in the shade from the wheel of the 4010 eating zamp pickle sandwiches with fat Oata Needarp? Are any of the farmers' *sons* here?

No sir, it's me, Yasch the oabeida.

Oata, Oata
Ossentoata

56

Penzel Panna made it up one day at recess time behind the girls' beckhouse while Oata was inside.

Pesst em Woata
Truff ein Koata

By dinner the whole school had learned it off by heart, even Pug Peters who couldn't learn the shortest Bible verse, "Jesus wept."

Truck sich dann bei Becksi oot
Funk doa einen brunen Kloot

The grade oners on the horse swings said it as they pumped and pulled.

Howd sich dann ne groute Frei
Docht dowt veah ein Ouster Ei

The girls with their braided binder twine ropes said it while they were skipping. Some that hide-and-go-seek played said it instead of telling numbers to a hundred.

Schmeickt seh eesht ein kleenet Beet
Yowma me dowt ess blous Sheet

Everywhere Oata went on the school yard we called out the Flat German verse to her. At first she tried some of the smaller ones to chase but she was then already 180 pounds so it was easy to run from her away. So Oata gave up and sat herself down by the big climbing sugar tree and looked to the church over the road. Her back was to us and she made like she didn't listen but every once in a while her shoulders would hop up and down and we could see she was onioning her eyes out.

I try to quietly chew the sandwich so that Oata can't nerk me for chewing loud and I don't say nothing, just look over the ripples of earth to the end of the field. I don't want to look at the three-cornered patch of creamfat ripples showing where Oata's shirt hangs down from the one button she has closed by her tits. I hear Oata chewing, then the tin scrapes on the glass when she screws off the lid from the jar of Freshie.

"Oata, Oata, Ossentoata," she says and I feel the bottom of the jar press into my hand. I have to look at her to take the jar.

> Pissed in the water
> Hit a catter

I get some Freshie into my Sunday throat and start to cough.

> Pulled herself the panties down
> Found a lump there nice and brown
> Thought it was a Easter egg
> Rolled it up and down her leg
> Tasted first a tiny bit
> Holy cow it is just shit

Oata's finger touches the flesh of my thumb and she takes the jar out from my hand.

"Nobody ever made up a verse about you, eh?" she says, then she laughers herself so that her whole front bobbers up and down. I say nothing, only look at the weeds on the part of the field that isn't diskered yet. A klunk of earth digs into my narsch and I wonder why I always get into such a pit. Then Oata says, "You made up the English one, didn't you?" I don't look at her but I can feel that brown eye mixing with the blue one and boring me through. Salt water leaks down the side of my ribs. "But then you are a Reimer on your mother's side, aren't you, Yasch?"

I look at my clock and see that it is time to get on with the seeding or I won't get back to Ha Ha Nickel's in time to play catch with Sadie before fire evening.

"I phoned to Ha Ha Nickel," Oata says just before I press the starter button. My hand freezes. "I said to him that you would stay here for supper so you can me to the hospital take to visit Futtachi. Ha Ha said it was okay, and said you should stay for night already. I...."

I press the button to drown her out and rev the engine up so that the diesel coming from the stack is so black that it matches the words from my mouth. And they don't rhyme neither, as I make that 4010 pull that disker through the field, make it struggle because that tractor is the only thing I can boss around. Everything else in the world bosses me around. It matters nothing what I want to do, there is always something to make me do what I don't want. The wind pushes an empty fertilizer sack over the summerfallow, shoves it from one klunk to another, waiting for a chance to chase it into a thorn bush or a barbed-wire fence.

I try to look my way around going to town with Oata but nothing for sure falls me by and when it is half seven already my stomach is hanging crooked and the fuel guage is showing empty. So I finish the round and hook loose the disker and drive to the yard and hold still by the diesel tank. Oata hurries herself out of the house as soon as the motor stops and I almost trip myself over the gearshift.

That such things one can see here on Nobah Naze Needarp's farm would I me not have thought even if the bull had farrowed. From a white elephant I had heard but here coming the yard across is Oata in a pink dress like a tent that would hold almost the Brunk Tent Crusade. She has her yellow brown gray hair tied up with a pink scarf and when she closer comes I can see her mouth is smeared with pink, too. Her pink in between the toes shoes with high heels yet dig in the ground, but when she stops and leans herself with her hand against the back tire of the 4010 all I can see is the little plastic pink butterflies screwed on her ears.

"Yasch, Yasch, hurry yourself up! The visiting hours start already at seven o'clock and you must yet eat and wash the summerfallow from yourself. Go behind the house. I put fresh water in the washcumb."

My ears still ring from the tractor motor and the words from those pink-smeared lips fly me by and then, even through the stink of the diesel and the grease, my nose sucks in a sinus-full of Evening in Schanzenfeld perfume and I proost so hard that one gob of mucus membrane sizzles on the muffler.

Half-warm water in the white washbowl with the red stripe around the rim. And lye soap with Evening in Schanzenfeld spritzed on it. I can't gribble it out if Oata is nerking me or trying too hard with 'limited resources' like the ag rep said at a 4-H meeting one time.

Oata sticks her head out from the green screen door of the ovenside and says she has made something hartsoft special for my supper, and I mutter to my chin that I hope it's not porridge with lots of salt like she used to make last year all the time. And it isn't. My faspa almost climbs up from my panz when she says, "It is today so hot that I thought you would like some Schmauntzup." I can hardly look at the big bowl of thick sour milk mixed up with green onions and cucumber. Muttachi used to make it for Futtachi and he would just shovel it down like it was the best treat in the world but I could never make myself eat it. I mean I don't even like to eat glumms, except when they are in verenichi.

So I look at the white clock with the red numbers that hangs by the chimney and say, "It's fifteen to seven already so we have to go or you'll for the visiting hours be late." I hurry the screen door out and Oata comes me after.

Nobah Naze's half-ton is still on the field with the seed so I flitz around the barn to the Ford tractor and hump spread-legged on to the seat. I push on the starter and there's only a click and when I reach for the key there's nothing in the key hole.

"Yasch, Yasch, not the tractor! We will the car take!"

The car? For sure, the car. Nobah Naze has a car. Only it is hard to remember it because he never drives it if he thinks there will be mud or dust. When I worked for him last year I saw it once just, in the ovenside of the chicken barn when we spent three hours in the middle of the best combining day of the harvest looking for the Jack-All. That was the one time I saw the dark green '51 Ford four-door, with white walls and radio yet, and one scratch just, so small you wouldn't see it except if Nobah Naze showed it to you, there by the 'R' in FORD on the trunk. Nobah Naze said to me that the bengels at church had scratched it the first Sunday when the car was new and so that's why he only the half-ton to church drives because the downixes like the preacher's son and the deacon's nephew play hookey from the church and fool around with people's cars while the elders are preaching and praying and holding the collect for wayward children's homes like Ailsa Craig. "Those church studs," he spit at me, "can see the flyshit in Ontario but they can't see the snudder which from their own nose leaks."

Oata is jingling the keys to the car by the ovenside door and I walk over trying to gribble out the consequentlies of taking Nobah Naze's pet car, knowing for sure that Nobah Naze will blame me even if it Oata's fault is. Oata has her door already open and throws me the keys over the roof before she squeezes herself into the woman's side and closes the door on her pink dress.

So sticks the fork in the handle, I think to myself, then I open the man's side and slide in behind the steer. For a moment I get a noseful of almost new car smell, then the Evening in Schanzenfeld drives out any other smells that might have been brave enough to even try to reek.

The car starts up like new and the gas guage shows three-fourths full and I figure I'll fill some gas up from the tank when

61

we get back. I slowly back out from the ovenside and as soon as I turn the car to the road Oata switches the radio on loud and CFAM sings into our ears but Oata cuts that out quick when she pushes the button to bring in Portage. The western music makes me to feel good, even if I had started to listen to the rock and roll because that is what Sadie Nickel likes. Somehow the guitars and banjos, fiddles and steel guitars touch me in the heart and make me feel churchy in a funny way, like when I was just a Jungchi with a brushcut and I used to go to Sunday Night Christian Endeavors because that's where the action was, and the girls would sit on the choir loft benches and their skirts would pull up a little over the knees and a guy could feel right happy to be in the church even if the children's story was just a little bit young and the gospel message was always too long. But the best part of it all was when the people in the choir who could play guitar would put those colored cords with the fuzzy tassels around their necks and put the picks on their thumbs or hold them between the fingers and line up behind the choir leader who had a hand plaything, and they would play old songs from the *Evangeliums* book and it would sound just like angels and the girls' fingers would scratch the picks over the strings and for days afterward I would make the sounds they made with my tongue
—DUNG DANG DANG, DUNG DANG DANG, DUNG
                    DUNG
                    DUNG
                            DUNG DANG DANG,
DUNG DANG DANG—
and sometimes Schallemboych Pete's bride from Sommerfeld would play her mandolin and go DWEET, DWEET, DWEET. But then they put up a wine-colored curtain fence in front of the choir loft so the girls' legs didn't show any more and the leader started to go to choir-leading schools in Winkler or someplace and learned such things as to have the choir people stand one behind the other and hit the person in the front with

the edge of your hand on the back at choir practice. And they stopped the guitars to play and only tried to sing such high music like Contatas and so I stayed home on Sunday nights if Muttachi would let me and listened to a States station which good country music had on Sunday nights.

And so now the radio has on good country songs all the way to the hospital except for one Ray Price song that I don't like the fiddle for and I guess even Oata doesn't like it because that's when she starts to talk with me and tells me not to be so shittery and drive a little faster. That makes me mad and when we reach the highway, I figure, let's see if this thing can squeal on pavement. I shift into low gear, rev up the motor and pop the clutch. The loose gravel squirts from the spinning tires and the rear end from the car swings to the side and when the rubber hits the pavement there is just a bit of a squeal and then the Ford shoots up to sixty real fast. I check the mirrors for a blue Ford that the Mounties use, then I floor the thing and the needle shoots up to eighty-five and the wind blows in through the vents and lifts up that pink dress like a tarp in a tornado and I can't help myself, I have to look at the creamfat white between the tops of the pink nylons and the pink elastic stuff that schneers into the soft skin under the garter. Oata doesn't bother herself to put the dress down and she just leans back in the seat with her elbow on the door handle that is like a little shelf. I had thought that maybe the speed would make her scared a little bit but she seems to like this going fast and she bounces one big round knee along with the guitars from an instrumental "Golden Wildwood Flower" and her big pink lips have half a smile on them and I make that Ford go even faster and when we get to the CFAM towers the needle is showing almost a hundred and Oata's lips are smiling so that her teeth are showing and her tent dress is blowing up in her face. Then she leans over and closes the window and the vent and the pink stuff falls down like a parachute and I take my foot off the footfeed and let the car

63

coast till we go just sixty and it's a good thing, too, because I am only going sixty for about half a minute when the blue Ford meets us on the curve that leads into town.

"The stripey gophers almost got you for showing off to a girl," she says and so I slow the car down to fifteen miles an hour and go slow like that till we are to the hospital.

Oata wobbles the hospital steps up on her spikes and I hunch myself down in the seat and hope that nobody will see me in Nobah Naze's car. Then I feel my stomach hanging crooked and so I go to the little store there beside the hospital and buy myself some Oh Henry bars and two bottles Wynola. Just when I'm going to walk out the little bell klingers on the door and in comes Tiedig Wiens's Mumchi who onetime best friends with Muttachi was and she talks me on and I have to talk her back. Tiedig Wienses used to be neighbors with us but now they live in town close to the hospital and the olden home so the Mumchi can better visit all those that are going dead. That's what she says me now, except that I know that Tiedig Wiens had his driving licence taken away and now he lives close enough to the parlor so that he can walk. Anyways, Tiedig Wiens's Mumchi tells me all about her boy, Melvin, who in Regina is learning to be an RCMP and that he likes it very much and it's easy for him because he's so smart, especially the taking care of the horses part. And I think about the time Melvin Wiens went to visit by Hingst Heinrichs's place on a Sunday after dinner and the boys decided to ride the old shrug that Heinrichs keeps for hauling the manure sled in winter. Now it took the shrug a little while to get the idea about what she was to do but by the time it was Melvin's turn she had it in her head that when something sat on her back she should run. The shrug took off as soon as Melvin climbed on and galloped him around the fence three times going faster and faster and Melvin was holding the rein on with both hands and yelling "Help! Help!" so loud that Hingst Heinrichs's sister (that Melvin really wanted to visit but didn't have the nerve for) came running to the barn just in time to see the shrug dump Melvin into the pig pen beside the fence and it had rained an inch the night before. Melvin Wiens was wearing his Sunday pants yet, too. Anyways, Tiedig Wiens's Mumchi says me again how happy she is to have such a nice boy who doesn't smoke and drink and who even to RCMP church goes on Sundays. Just then the storeman's cuckoo clock goes off and the old lady lets me get away without saying her anything about myself or Muttachi.

I go back to the car and eat my stuff while the sun glances off the hospital windows and the shadows get longer. The Wynola bottles get empty and I feel still thirsty and I gribble in my head if I should quickly drive to the hotel and pick up a six. But then Oata comes out the door where the sun isn't glancing off the glass any more and I watch her come down the big steps with her pink dress.

"Take me to the Dairy Dell for soft ice cream," says Oata when she has sat herself back in the car.

Now the Dairy Dell was where I wanted to take Sadie Nickel after the ball game against Panzenfeld last Sunday only she left me before the game over was because that snuddernose Pug Peters was taking her to the "Town Without Pity" show in Neche. The Dairy Dell is the place where everybody goes in the summer time after anything is over and there is always somebody there that knows you and will come to talk you on, for sure if you have a woman along. I mean it's always that way on Sunday nights if you are lucky enough or brave enough when you are driving through all the darps or up and down the main street to hold still by some girls that are walking the road along and you find enough nerves to talk them on in a nice way and sometimes you get full of luck and they will get in the car and you can go driving the sunflower fields through on the middle roads but you always go to the Dairy Dell before the night is over. And at the Dairy Dell all those that didn't pick up some girls crowd the cars around where the girls are in and so I sure don't feel like going there with Oata in Nobah Naze's car.

But it is Monday evening and when we get to the Dairy Dell there just is one big truck and it doesn't look like it matters so I park the car close to the shack so that Oata can see the food list that's painted on the side. Besides, I didn't eat any supper. I ask Oata what she wants and she says, "Just soft ice cream," and so I go to the window and tell Trudy Teichroeb's mom that I want a soft ice cream and a nip and a milkshake. Then I lean myself on the shelf that they have by the window and look at the truck and see one beard, one polka dotted kerchief, and two little boys with suspenders. Just some Huttatolas eating soft ice cream.

My food is ready and I pay for it and I think I will be lucky enough to get from the Dairy Dell away before somebody sees me but no such luck. I am just passing Oata's ice cream through the window to her when Pug Peters and Hingst Heinrichs come skidding into the yard and throw dust over everything. I hurry myself into the car and shove the milkshake and nip to Oata and say "Hold this!" and I let loose the car and peel out from that yard.

But it is already too late. Those dipsticks make a U-ball and come us after down the 14A. Oata hollers, "HOLEM DE GRUEL!" and rutches herself over to the middle of the seat so that her side is leaning me against. Just what I yet need when I want to go as fast as the Ford can and I have to steer with both hands and Oata is leaning me against so that my arm is clamped in between my ribs and her lard but I floor that thing anyway and Oata counts along with the red needle: 65 70 75 80 85 90 95 100 and I look in the mirror behind and I can see Hingst's car is getting closer and I step harder even if the pedal is flat on the floor already but the needle stays there just by hundred. And then I see it.

"LOOK, YASCH!"

The gray Vauxhall creeps the white line along, five 'n twenty miles an hour just like always and I know that Happy

Heppner's grandfather is driving his Mumchi around again. But then I see in the other lane coming us on from the front a big yellow combine, and another one behind and another and another and another. Five new Cockshutt combines creeping us towards and I know for sure that Nobah Naze's '51 Ford better have good brakes or me and Oata will have to make a detour through the ditch.

Oata just leans herself closer to me and licks her ice cream when the rubber starts to squeal and the car wags its tail a little but I manage to make the Ford stop the Vauxhall five feet behind, just when the first combine is even with it. Happy Heppner's grandfather keeps just on driving and I don't think he noticed us *or* the combines. Burned rubber smell drowns out the Evening in Schanzenfeld perfume and at the same time there is loud honking behind and I know that Hingst and Pug have caught up.

I put the car back in gear and creep after the gray Vauxhall and those penzels behind us keep blowing their horn and Oata leans her head on my shoulder yet and bites off the side of the cone, but then I see my chance because the last combine is farther behind than the other ones so I floor that Ford and whip it around the Vauxhall and shoot away.

"Yippy Doodles!" yells Oata and she turns herself around to look out the back and she shteepas herself with her hand on my leg a little bit too close to the intersection for me right now because I have the footfeed flat on the floor again trying to get as far as I can before Pug gets by those combines. Well, I'm going 95 again when Oata pinches me on the leg and her chin is leaning on my shoulder and her hair is making my ear itchy and she yells, "They made it around!" So I jerk myself frontward to make that car go faster and then for sure her hand is in the wrong place and I see some lights coming from the front but I am going 100 now and then I think that I don't have my lights on but it is already too late—the car that is coming on is blinking a red light already. For a few seconds my foot stays flat on the floor, then I take it off the gas and shove Oata out of the way a little and switch the lights on. I let the car coast till it's just going 50, then I hold it there but the blinking red light is already turning around behind us and I can hear the siren.

Oata doesn't say nothing while we wait for the police to come to the car. Then the police is there and I can see from his thin shnuitsboat that it is the same police that held me up one other time and he looked all through the half-ton cab with his flashlight but he couldn't find nothing and I got away with having a 24 of States beer under the hood.

"You were driving without your lights on," he says to me.

"Well, it wasn't yet altogether dark."

"You were traveling pretty fast, too." I don't say nothing but I know now that he doesn't know for sure how fast I was going. Then he wants to see my driver's and the car registration. He looks them on for a minute, then he leans his head in the window as far as his hat will let him and he says to Oata, "This your father's car?"

"Yeah," says Oata.

"Do you have a driver's licence?"

"Yeah, sure," she says, and she starts to stir around in her purse and she pulls out a driver's licence and I wonder me what the hund I am doing here when Oata could have easy driven herself to the hospital and I could have gone back to Ha Ha's and played catch with Sadie Nickel at fire evening. Just then a car drives slowly past and I hear Hingst Heinrichs yell, "PAUSS UP WITH NOBAH NAZE'S CAR!" My ears are sure hot and they get hotter yet when the police reaches Oata's driver's and the registration through the window to her and he says, "Why don't you drive your father's car home before show-off here has an accident?"

"Okay," she says, and the police opens my door. What can a guy do? I get out and Oata rutches herself behind the steer. The police looks my driver's on a little bit more.

"Aren't you getting a bit old for these tricks?" He lets his eyes bore at me from under the hat, then he gives me back my driver's and stands there watching while I creep into Nobah Naze's car on the woman's side.

Oata starts up the car and grinds it into low gear. Then she gives it gas before she lets the clutch out and the tires spin in the dirt beside the pavement and she stalls the motor. I look back and see the police standing there and I can see he is laughering himself. Oata tries again and this time she gets the car going except she doesn't shift out from low gear and the car is making lots of noise so I say, "Shift gears already." Oata steps on the clutch but she keeps her foot on the throttle and the motor revs like crazy but she gets it into second and we go like that till we get to the turn-off corner. This time she remembers to shift gears and then she even goes fast enough to need high gear so I tell her to shift again.

"Eat your nip already," she says. "Soon it will be cold."

The nip is cold, but I eat it. Oata doesn't say nothing else, she just drives and all of a sudden I'm thinking about the time when I was 10 years old and we had just moved to Gutenthal from Yanzeed, where my Futtachi was working out for a farmer by Chortitz. 'Handy as in Chortitz' the people always said but it wasn't handy for us even if you could back up with the harrow. So Futtachi moved us to Gutenthal and for a whole year in school the other guys always ran from me away. Every time I came close they would run and hide and then say things to nerk me from behind the trees. It didn't feel so good to always be run away from and when Oata quietly says I shouldn't forget to drink the milkshake I don't feel so good about the things we used to do to her in school.

It is dark already when we get to Nobah Naze's place and it suddenly falls me by that Oata hasn't said nothing about her Futtachi, if he is very sick or not. So I ask her and she just says, "Not so good," and she turns the radio louder because the song is about the old log cabin for sale.

69

The yard is very still and the moon is coming up over the willow trees by the waterhole where the frogs are having choir practice and I think about the time when it was forty degrees cold and Schacht Schulz brought his tape recording machine to school and played us some frog singing that he had taped by Buffalo Creek and he thought it would warm us up to hear frogs on such a cold day. And while we were listening Irene Olfert was looking back to me with her little mirror and I got this tickling feeling in my bones and I thought it would be nice to sit on a waterhole hump with her and listen to real frogs in the summertime but when summertime came the Olferts had moved to Ontario to pick tomatoes.

Now Oata makes the door open to the house and I start to wonder me what I am doing following her to the house when I should be walking to my Muttachi's place for the night. It would be only a mile and a half across the field. Or I could even the tractor take and then come back in the morning to finish the seeding.

"Make the door closed. The mosquitoes are coming in."

So I do it and I stand there in the kitchen and the lights aren't switched on and it falls me by that Nobah Naze hardly ever used the hydro at night in the summertime because he said too many flies come to the house when the lights are on. Now it doesn't seem such a silly idea after all, even if by Ha Ha Nickel's they have a yellow bulb outside by the porch door that is supposed to keep the bugs away. And anyways if the mosquitoes get bad Ha Ha just lights on some do-do coils, which is like having mosquito smoke, only it is handier, and stinks a little like perfume.

But here now in Nobah Naze's kitchen it is dark except for one slice of moonshine that through the little window over the cook oven shines on the Elephant Brand fertilizer calendar, and the Evening in Schanzenfeld is still strong enough so we don't need any do-do coils. Oata steps into the streak of moonshine and her eyes blitz a little and the rhinestones on her butterfly

70

earrings glance the light off like snow on a Christmas card. The pink dress fuschels as she goes to the cupboard and reaches the oil lamp and puts it on the table. Then she sticks her hand inside her dress by the shoulder and pulls a strap straight. "Light on the lamp, and I'll get us something to drink," Oata says and she turns on her high heels so that the dress swings around and she takes two steps then she bends over and lifts the ring in the floor and opens the lid to the cellar. The pink tent sinks down the steps and I take the chimney off the oil lamp and turn the little wheel so the wick comes up. Then I take a farmer match from the little tin holder on the wall by the stove and I light on the lamp. The lamplight makes the room darker because the flame chases the moonshine away and all the shadows are big from everything that is away from the table. I sit myself down on one of the chairs without thinking and feel right away that it is the chair with the crack in it and when I move my ham I get a pinch. So I take a different chair and sit there looking at the lamp and listen to a cricket that is fiddling away somewhere in the house. Everything is still. Even from the cellar I can't hear Oata, and I think a little bit that it would be nice if it was Sadie in the cellar, but then I remember that Sadie went to the "Town Without Pity" show with Pug Peters on Sunday, and it doesn't seem so nice if Sadie was in the cellar.

Some glass clinks down there and then creak the steps and I watch past the lamp as Oata rises from the hole in the floor. The flame from the oil lamp makes shadows on the pink dress and in her hands she holds a big catsup bottle but it sure isn't catsup that is in it. Oata sets the catsup bottle on the table beside the lamp and she goes over to the cupboard and gets out two glasses with handles, the kind you can buy peanut butter in, and she puts them down beside the lamp. Then she tries to pull the cork out from the catsup bottle but it won't come loose so she reaches it to me and I try to wiggle it but it is real tight so I put the bottle between my knees to get a better grip and then the cork starts to move and out it comes with a pop.

I reach the bottle back to Oata and she pours one glass half full and then the other one and it looks real pretty there with the flame from the lamp showing through. Oata pushes one glass over the table to me, then she sits down and lifts the other glass with the handle. I lift my glass, too, and she reaches over her glass so it clinks with mine. Then she pulls the glass to her pink lips and takes a sip. Some of the pink stays on the glass when she puts it back on the table beside the lamp. I take a sip, too, and the chokecherry wine tastes a little shtroof on my tongue but it's good and I take another sip, too.

"Pretty good, huh, Yasch?" I wobble my head up and down and take another sip. "I made it myself."

Everything is still, except the cricket is playing the fiddle some place. And the white clock with the red numbers is ticking with that sound that always makes me think about a rocking chair. Every sip from the wine is better than the one before and mixed with the chokecherry smell the Evening in Schanzenfeld is quite nice and Oata's pink fingernails sparkle when they reach around the catsup bottle to pour us some more wine and the rhinestones in her butterfly earrings glitter when she laughs. I say, "It's good that your Foda buys catsup in such big bottles." Oata smiles and sips a little more wine and then she licks the spitz of her tongue around those pink lips and the lamplight funkles in her brown eye and then in her blue eye and I start to think some place in my head that it is maybe something special to have a blue eye and a brown eye and I wonder if the world looks better with a blue eye or a brown eye and then Oata says, "Yasch, you have pink eyes!"

And I know for sure that I have a pink face because the stubble on my chin feels hot and Oata rutches her chair closer to me so she can pour the last wine from the catsup bottle into our glasses and as she holds the bottle so that the last drops of the chokecherry wine can leak into my glass she is leaning close by me and at first the Evening in Schanzenfeld is real strong again but then the nose starts to pick up something else, like if the wine and the perfume and Oata got mixed up together into one sweet blooming garden of stickroses, tea blooms, butterflowers, and sweet clover in a hay loft. And Oata clinks her glass to mine again and we both take just a little sip to make it last longer and a drop runs over her pink bottom lip and I think for sure that it shouldn't go to waste and I lean over and stick my tongue out to catch it and Oata rutches her chair closer and we share the last drops from the glasses and Oata says, "I forgot the lid to close," and she starts to stand up and I say, "I will for you it close," and we are standing both beside the cellar lid and I bend over and make it closed. Then Oata leans on me and I have to shteepa myself against the door frame that leads into the sitting room and the next thing we are in the moonshine on the wine-colored sofa with the big flowers all over it and I am driving the double dike along in a big rain with the big ditch between the dike and Nobah Naze's half section and the half-ton is schwaecksing from side to side on the slippery mud and the canal is half full with water and I am turning the steer from one side to the other as fast as I can and the truck plows through a deep mud puddle and the windshield is smattered full and I can't see nothing and the wipers only schmaus it fuller and I can say for sure that looks matter nothing and the tires feel the slippery road over a hump and I try the brakes to use but the truck is going already down and it is too late to be afraid of anything there could be to see and I just let myself feel what there is to know. Then the truck stops and the motor sputters and dies and I can hear my heart hammering away like an old John Deere two-cylinder driving along in road gear. I feel the water seepering in through the floor of the truck. But I just sit there till the water starts to leak into my boots and I turn and look out the window on the woman's side of the cab and I see the wild mustard blooming on Nobah Naze's field.

Then there is ringing in my ears like a saw blade hitting a nail in an old fence pole and Oata pushes me away and schluffs off to the phone with her pink stockings on her feet just. I hear her say "Hello" and "Yes" and "Oh" and then "Oh" again. Oata comes slowly back into the moonshine by the sofa. She steps on a pink shoe and she falls me beside on the bench. I take her around with my arms and she leans her head on my chest. I stroke her hair a little and she starts to shudder. Then the tears let go and I feel them when they run off from her cheek into the hairs on my belly. And there is nothing to say. Nothing to see. Just to feel. Nobah Naze Needarp is dead.

Chapter Six

I should have clawed out from there fast, I guess, maybe to Mexico or Thompson even. I mean, I could see it already then, there in the morningshine on the wine sofa with the pink tent dress crumpled on the floor by the pink high heels. Outside in the garden a mourning dove cooed again and again and again, and Oata's head was warm on my chest and hot tears leaked in the circle of eleven hairs by my navel. A man can't just claw out from a woman like that, at least not if she has just found out that her Futtachi has gone dead. I mean if a person goes dead you can't just turn away and spin your tires. Not if you want to call yourself a mensch. A mensch has to deal with other mensch and when you try to do something with another mensch it always gets kompliziet. And when you try to do something with a fruemensch it can be like building a fence with hackel-wire you found at the mist-acre. But that's the ball game.

For sure, it's no trouble to play catch with yourself. Just throw the ball straight up and it falls always right in your glove back. And in your head you can dream that such a good ball player you are. And you never miss because even if you throw a curve you know how it's coming for you heaved it yourself. And you can play catch with yourself anytime you feel like it because you are always ready and you don't have to wait for nobody to find their gloves or their baseball caps. And you can play catch with yourself any place, even on the field on the tractor by holding the steer between your knees. But it gets kind of lonesome and one day you think this is no way to raise a family and you start to look for someone to play catch with even if it means that you only can play catch when the other person wants to play, too. And then you can't control the game so easy no more because the other person sometimes misses your best pitch, or throws you back a wild one that smashes a window. But the worst is when you are really hot about the game but the other person doesn't feel like it and so throws the ball that it doesn't to you all the way come. But it is better than catch all by yourself.

Yep, I should have clawed out from there fast like a '57 Chev but Oata's head was on my chest, her shoulder leaning on my ribs, and her pillowy breast was warming my belly through the pink underskirt. And if a Futtachi goes dead it is like somebody hacked off a big tree that you were gripping on in a windstorm and now you have to shteepa yourself on something else. Going dead is such a weighty thing that you have to lean on someone else even if the load you share with them is uncomfortable. For sure, Oata was quite a load, but comfortable she was like a heavy quilt on a restless night that presses you down and pushes your muscles and nerves into place and makes them hold still. And then the mourning dove sang its song again like Hank Williams when he sings "I'm so lonesome I could cry" and I thought about Sadie Nickel and the "Town Without Pity" show and playing catch with her at fire evening and how she could always my pitches catch and she was like a willow in the wind. And about my plan to maybe rent some land and try to make something from myself. And I wanted to claw out from there. But then I looked past Oata's hair, out the sitting room window and I saw the double dike and the wild mustard blooming on Nobah Naze's field. Somebody would have to take care of Oata's mustard.

It didn't take Oata long to figure out what to do with me. First I had to drive her to the hospital again, where she made me go with to see her Foda and I felt real embarrassed going after her into the front door from the hospital and she still had on the pink dress only she put a black coat on over it and I had on my field clothes and then yet the nurse at the front was my Muttachi's second cousin from Yanzeed who is such a pluida zack that I knew for sure that before the sun went down me and Oata would be married with thirteen grandchildren.

I don't like dead people to see. Sure, Futtachi always said that the dead ones can't do you nothing. With the live ones you must watch out. Still, I was for sure not happy to look at Nobah Naze there on the white hospital bed with the side fences all the way up and just one eye closed. Oata held herself on the side fence so tight that her fingernails were white even through the pink nail polish. And I couldn't look at Nobah Naze no more because his open eye was boring me through and so I looked at Oata and she was biting her lip trying to hold something in. And I did what I always see other people do at funerals: I put my hand on her shoulder and it felt like the right thing to do. Oata bit harder and then the dike gave and tears flooded over the round cheeks through the red powdery stuff that was still there from last evening. And I thought about what my Muttachi always says when she from a funeral home comes that it is good to let the tears run when somebody goes dead because then it doesn't hurt so much. It was good, I thought, for Oata to cry.

Muttachi's nurse cousin from Yanzeed then came us by and said to us that they had to take Nobah Naze to autopsy if Oata would the paper sign and she looked me one on so that I knew I shouldn't go with that time.

I was for sure glad to claw from that bed away with the open eye and I was almost the hospital door out when I thought I should maybe for Oata wait. So I sat down in the waiting room and picked up one of those doctor magazines that was there and started to page it through. That was when I saw it and it was like there was ice poking up and down my backstring and my heart started to clapper so fast and so hard I thought it would smash my ribs right through. And I got so cold, cold like Nobah Naze himself, and I felt black like there was dirty oil running me through instead of blood. I tried to think myself away from it, so much angst I had, but the words burned me into the head so much that I had to read the whole page even if it was full of high doctor words. The doctor words alone weren't so gruelich but when my head mixed them together with two hundred pounds of Oata, half a section wild mustard, and my fifteen-year-old willow, Sadie, it came out like sticky tar, and it wouldn't let loose.

Now there is mud on my black Sunday shoes that I smeared with Skuff-Kote so they would look almost new. And there is some mud on the black pants, too, from Futtachi's old Sunday suit that Muttachi took the pants in for me so I could be usher at Nobah Naze's funeral.

It has to rain for Nobah Naze. I mean, I think Nobah Naze would have liked it like this. And he would be real shtollt to know what Oata has done and he would be laughering himself behind his hand. Yes sir, it's like the weather can sometimes feel along with how people feel. You know, on Still Friday when Jesus is nailed on the cross it often rains and is cold and windy; then on Easter it is sunshine and warm. Sure Nobah Naze Needarp would frei himself at this rain, not just because I got the seeding finished while Oata was making the funeral ready. Not just because they let his Mumchi home to the funeral from the mental hospital, with two big nurses walking her between them, even after when Oata phoned to the hospital to tell her Muttachi that Nobah Naze was gone dead and then the next day the nurse phoned Oata back and said maybe her Muttachi wouldn't be let to come to the funeral because when they told Mumchi Needarp that her Omchi had gone dead she had started to dance around and tear her clothes from off herself and shout "Hallelujah!" And Oata was feeling real bad about this but she said to me that if she her mother was, she would shout "Hallelujah!", too, because if Nobah Naze hadn't been so scared that another man would look her on she would never have had to go to the mental home. Oata told me that her mother had said to her what had happened when her parents got married. People still did old-fashioned things then, and in the evening after the wedding the young people and the bride and groom would go to the school yard and play singing games. It was a little bit like dancing and all the men were in a circle and all the women were in another circle inside the men's circle and they would sing and go around and when the singing stopped the man would take the girl that stopped him beside around with his arm and walk with her till the singing stopped again. And Oata's mother was having fun and Nobah Naze could hear her laughing and he started really jealous to get. And then when the game over was and it was already dark Nobah Naze couldn't find his bride. He looked the school yard all over but she wasn't anywhere. And the people went away and Nobah Naze was there all alone. Then a Model A came in the school yard and somebody shouted, "Hey, Nobah Naze, what is loose with you? Your bride is waiting already for you at home!" Nobah Naze walked across the field home and his bride was there sitting on the steps because those guys had chained shut the door and she couldn't get in, but she was happy and still laughing even when her bride dress was all wet from the grass at the bottom. And Nobah Naze was so mad that he wouldn't sleep in the same bed that night and he always made her stay home and wouldn't hardly even let her to church go. And even if he took her along someplace she had to right beside him stay and if another man tried to talk her on, or even looked her on more than one time, he would right away hurry her to the car and drive home. Nobah Naze wouldn't let her go to sewing circle or help at weddings or anything like that, and even when Oata was born he still couldn't forget and he would sometimes hold the baby up and say, "Are you really my baby? I wonder." And so Oata's mother started to do strange things and when Oata was nine years old her mother went to the mental home. Oata was happy that her mother to the funeral could come and maybe Nobah Naze would have been happy, too.

But I think what would have freid Nobah Naze the most would have been to see Milyoon Moates slip through the yellow lime of the church yard with his eighty dollar shoes. And to see A.M. Kuhl and his later brother P.M. Kuhl huff and puff in their striped suits with frilly shirts. And Yelttausch Yeeatze, Rape Rampel, and Barley King Barkman all almost letting the coffin slip from off the hearse. And in school we always thought maybe Oata wasn't all there. I mean, who would have thought that the Credit Committee from the Credit Union would be pall bearers for Nobah Naze Needarp? Never had I heard Nobah Naze say one good thing about the Credit Committee. I mean, only last winter in the store I heard him swear out the Credit Committee from bottom to top and then around a little bit yet because he wanted to buy another half section land from Gevitta Ginter's widow but the Credit Committee wouldn't the loan approve even when he got two co-signers. And then the next day we all heard that the Kuhl brothers had bought one quarter and Rape Rampel the other. So I drove almost the road off when Oata told me that she would ask these guys to carry her father to his grave. For sure you can't say no when somebody asks you to be a pall bearer.

For sure not if they say, "It was his wish." And so the Credit Committee from the Credit Union did what they didn't want to let the Credit Union do, they carried him to his new land.

Yes sir, everyone came to take Nobah Naze under. People that wouldn't give him the wax from their ears when he still lived came to see him when he was dead. Maybe it was because of the rain and the farmers couldn't do nothing on the field, but when the undertaker made the coffin open so that the people could see Nobah Naze one more time, it seemed like it would take till milking time before the long line of people going past to look would be at the end. And they didn't look just. They all had a handshake with Nobah Naze's Mumchi, who sat those big nurses between and wobbled her head to each new person, and with Oata who sat them beside. Oata cried just about every time when a fresh person came and I was happy for sure that I was usher and could stand in the back. The way Oata nutzed me out while she was making the funeral ready I thought for sure she would make me sit in the front with her, but I just had to drive the hearse behind with the '51 Ford and be usher.

To be usher by this funeral was a real job because the church was soon full and then the upstairs part was full and even the choir loft was full. It laughered me a little that Hingst Heinrichs and Pug Peters had to sit in the loft where everybody could see them. Even the cellar was full with people and I had to tell Lectric Loewen to turn the loudspeaking box on so people could hear down there, too.

It was a long funeral. I mean it was as long as the time when the reeve died. Oata got Preacher Funk to preach in German and that was a long one, so long that the people were shrugging their hind ends on the benches already and blowing more noses than when everybody had a cold. Then Preacher Janzen preached in English, and the people sat a little stiller because Janzen was one of those that had learned himself to preach in the States, and you know how the States people always have to make a big show out of everything, just like they were living on TV. So he waved his arms and prayed three times before he started to preach. And then he preached everything he knew from Adam and Eve to the time when all the good people will marry with Jesus. And he talked about sin and he hammered his fist on the pulpit and I thought about the chokecherry wine and Oata with the pink dress on the floor and I had again the black thoughts that I felt when I read the stuff in the magazine in the hospital. And then my belly started to make noises and I thought about all the buns and cheese in the church cellar, and the sugar cubes, too. Oata sent me to pick the buns up from the bakery yesterday and I put them in the church cellar myself and so I didn't hear everything the English preacher said, which is not bad I guess, because my head was already so full with thinking that I was a headache starting to get. And my necktie was schneering my throat so tight I could almost not swallow my spit. But then Preacher Jansen prayed again, and he had his arms spread out like angel wings, and he said a long prayer and then Klaviera Klassen started the piano to play, slowly, and Preacher Funk said in Flat German that all the people were loaded in for something to eat after the family came back from the church yard. And then the undertaker shoved Nobah Naze around a little bit so the people could look at him.

But the best Oata has saved for the grave. The coffin is hanging on those straps that the undertaker puts over the hole and the people are standing around, some even standing on the rug that is almost like green grass, getting yellow mud on it because it is still raining, and Zamp Pickle Peters makes a Flat German speech. Now, Zamp Pickle Peters comes from the wrong side of the double dike just like the rest of us and he always tells it like he believes it. And he doesn't do it different this time. He says what he thinks. He says Nobah Naze had been like a stone that was trying to roll up the side of the dike. And every time he got close to the top, people would push him and then he would roll into the ditch back. But, he says, now all that is to the end. Nobah Naze is gone where it doesn't matter if your wild oats have grown better than your wheat. Or if your tractor is old and your plow tied together with hackel-wire. God doesn't care if you have manure on your four-buckles. For God such a man is just as good as the man who has two sections all himself and a brand new Versatile four-wheel drive. And then Zamp Pickle stops for blowing his nose. People start to fuschel but they hurry stop when he starts to talk again. And he says that people often laughered themselves at Nobah Naze because Nobah Naze was like a soldot that didn't march in the same step with the others. For sure it is nice when everybody marches with the same step. It all goes smooth then and even. But what happens when the soldoten all march together with the same step and they over a bridge go? The bridge crashes down. Nobah Naze helped us to keep from crashing the bridges through, and we laughered ourselves over him. Now we are here together to dig him under. How come we can love the dead ones better than the living ones?

And then Zamp Pickle Peters can't hold the salt water back and he covers his face with his hat. Preacher Funk starts to sing "Nun Danket Aller Gott" and the people sing with. The undertaker makes the lid closed on the coffin and he pushes the button that lets Nobah Naze down into the ground. It starts to rain more and all of a sudden Nobah Naze's Mumchi breaks from the big nurses away and she runs up the muddy pile of alkali, takes the space that is stuck there, and starts to shovel full the grave. The people stand there all bedoozled and then she laughs and laughs like a baby that has never before laughed. Oata tries to climb up to her but her black high heels sink into the mud and then the two big nurses grab Oata's Muttachi and lead her to a car.

Oata then looks me on and I can't help myself. I go to her and take her arm and help her to Nobah Naze's car. It matters nothing if Hingst Heinrichs and Pug Peters and the rest of the ball team can see me. It matters nothing that Sadie Nickel is standing her mother beside. It matters nothing at all.

I drive Oata slowly back to the church and she doesn't say nothing, just looks the window out. Then when I hold the car still in front by the church she says, "Sit with me to eat." And so I go in the cellar with her and sit beside her at the middle table, and all the people that didn't to the grave go look us on and then fuschel to themselves.

Soon the cellar is full with people and the preachers are sitting at the middle table with us and Preacher Funk stands up and is going to say the Dank for the food when one of the big nurses comes in and leans over to Oata and quietly says to her that she should come out and say goodbye to her mother because she is too sick to stay some more by the funeral. So Oata says to Preacher Funk that he should say the Dank. When the preacher has finished the people start to eat and talk and Oata pokes me in the ribs and fuschels that I am supposed to come with. So we go out from the cellar without eating nothing and go out to the nurse's car. Nobah Naze's wife is sitting in the back seat with the other nurse and she isn't laughing now. She just looks very tired and like she doesn't know nothing no more. The nurse makes the door open and Oata sits in the seat with her Muttachi. Oata takes her mother by the hand and then she gives her mother a kiss on the cheek. Her mother takes her around with her arm and they squeeze each other tight and then they both cry.

The nurse that drives the car stands there and watches a little bit then she says to me that I should Oata take to the hospital to see her mother often and that would help her to get better. Then she sticks her head in the open car door and touches Oata on the shoulder and says that they have to go now. So Oata kisses her mother one last time and she comes out. Oata stands and looks after the car till it goes the corner around and

84

then she pulls me on the sleeve and says, "I want to go home." So I open the woman's door on Nobah Naze's car and Oata creeps in. I don't even ask anything about the people that are eating her buns and cheese in the church cellar. I know how she feels, because when my Futtachi didn't come back from Mexico I wanted to be away from all the people, too.

The road to Nobah Naze's place is quite slippery now with all the rain but the '51 Ford is a good car and I can drive through the mud and only schwaecks once in a while. Oata is very still and I stay still, too. I don't switch even the radio on. I just drive, slow. When I turn the car in by Nobah Naze's long driveway I have to step on the footfeed because Nobah Naze never put gravel on and the tracks are soft from all the rain. But we make it through and I hold the car still in front by the house. I get out and hold open the door for Oata. She stops by the mudscraper that is cemented into a tire there by the plank that leads to the door and claws some of the mud from her high heels. Then she turns to me and says, "Put the car in the ovenside."

So I drive in to the ovenside by the chicken barn where Nobah Naze always the car parked and I turn the key off and just sit there trying to gribble out what I am going to do. I think about Nobah Naze's half section that I have just finished seeding for Oata. Sure with just a little bit digging I could easy lead the water puddles off into the ditches and then it wouldn't take so long in the spring before the land could be acred. The land would be good to have. It would give me the chance to get ahead because Futtachi never had nothing to give me a start like the other farmers' sons. But to marry with Oata Needarp to get some land. That is quite something. But it wasn't so bad with Oata in the pink dress and with the chokecherry wine. I mean lots of men get married with thin women and then soon they are fat, too. But fat like Oata? Could skinny Sadie Nickel ever get fat like Oata? Not that fat. And I think about what it said in that doctor magazine, that people that are terribly fat don't have long to live, that people that are two hundred pounds before they are twenty don't often live till they are twenty-five. And Oata is almost twenty. And Sadie fifteen. And I think about the plan I had reckoned out in my head when I was working by Ha Ha Nickel's, about how I would rent some land if Ha Ha would co-sign for me and then when Sadie was old enough we could get married and I could be a big shot farmer like her old man and I could play catch with my little willow Sadie all I want. My back-string shivers now when I think about this other black way there might be to get what I want. Could I do such a thing, marry Oata for her land and wait for her to go dead from fat? Yasch, Yasch, you are a real black one, I say to myself, but the idea pinches into my head like Nobah Naze's cracked chair in the kitchen pinches into narsch when you sit on it. And again I want to claw out from there, away from this sticky tar and just play ball and haul out twenty-fours from the hotel and drink beer in my old half-ton beside the big ditch that cuts us off from the States.

Then it falls me by that my half-ton is still by Ha Ha Nickel's and that I haven't seen it after Ha Ha sent me to seed for Nobah Naze. I climb out from the car and look out through the ovenside door. Dunner and blitzen it is raining hartsoft again and I can hardly see to the house from the barn. For sure I can't walk the mile and a half to my Muttachi's place in this. So I run as fast as I can to Oata's door. But when I open the door I am already rained right through to my skin.

I stand there on the rag rug by the door and the water leaks off from Futtachi's old Sunday suit. From the sitting room I can hear playing the piano. Oata is playing a song from her correspondence piano lessons that she always played last year when I worked out by Nobah Naze. She can play it better now, but she still gets the time a little bit wrong. When she finishes the song I hear the piano bench rutch on the floor and then she is standing in the door. She has her black funeral dress taken off and she is just in her black underskirt with her black stockings.

86

"Yasch, all wet you are! Pull yourself all out and I'll get you something dry." Oata shluffs over the floor with her nylons and goes up the stairs making the whole house creak. I start to pull myself out and when I have my pants off Oata calls, "Leave your wet stuff down there and come up here."

So I go up, and Oata has laid herself on the bed in her room. The green roll curtain is pulled down and it is almost dark like the night in there.

"Come, sit on the bed," she says quietly. And I do and she puts her hand on my arm. She rubs the tips from her fingers over my arm real soft. Then she says, "I'm all alone now. Nobody cares. Except maybe you." I say nothing and think she will ask next, "Do you?" but she doesn't. She just rubs my arm some more. Then her nylon is touching my leg and I put my hand on hers. "Lie down on the bed and hold me," she says, so quiet I almost don't hear. So I lie down on the bed and stretch my arm out so that Oata can put her head on my chest and I stroke her hair. She closes her eyes and her body is warm against mine. She doesn't cry. She starts to sleep, and then she snores a little. She starts to get a little heavy on my ribs but I don't want to wake her and my black plan marches through my head again, but Oata is warm, and I see Sadie stretching and jumping to catch a wild pitch from me and the plan doesn't seem quite so black and Oata snores louder and so even that soon I sleep, too.

The bell from the farmer phone rings two long and one short. Then again. And again, only this time it cranks two very long ones and then a short one and Oata squirms from off my chest and she says, "Yasch, go and see who it is." So I go down the steps to the farmer phone and it is my Muttachi.

"Yasch, Yasch, what is loose with you? It is late already, almost half eleven! What are you still doing over by Oata's? What the people will say? Get your narsch home now, or I'll with the flyclapper come!"

Muttachi talks on and on and won't let me say one word so I blow into the talking part from the phone and it tickles her in the ear. She stops and I hurry say, "Muttachi! How come you all of a sudden now worry yourself over what the people will say? You want me to leave a poor girl all by her lonesome when we just had to dig her Futtachi under and her Muttachi is in the mental home? Is that how the Bible says you should love your neighbor? Just go to sleep Muttachi!"

I quickly hang the phone up, then I find some paper and stick it between the two bells so the clapper can't ring and I go back up stairs.

Chapter Seven

I have to hook on by Muttachi's place and I don't feel so good. Oata chased me out from the bed and she didn't seem at all happy that I was there. And when I tickled her roll of fat by her belly while she was standing there by the washing up pan, she threw the tubdewk at me and hit me right in the face.

"Go away and don't come back!" she said, and I wonder how come a woman can change so much from the evening to the morning. And everything I did for her, too! Taking her to town, picking up the buns, usher at the funeral, and last evening yet after Muttachi phoned at half-eleven I go out to milk the cows. Now for sure I am the laughing stockade of the ball team. But I have go to to Muttachi and get some other clothes on because I can't go back to work by Ha Ha Nickel's if I have on my Futtachi's old Sunday suit that Muttachi fixed up for me so I could be usher at the funeral.

And I know Muttachi will be mad at me because I didn't come home, and she knows where I was. When you have been the night with a girl you don't want your mother in the morning to see. For sure not if the girl is mad at you, too. It makes it feel a little bit like sin, what felt so good before. But Ha Ha and Sadie would laugher themselves silly if I came with the black suit. They will laugher themselves enough already when I come on foot because my half-ton is still there. I almost go back to Oata's door to see if I can use Nobah Naze's car that I was driving Oata around with. But that would laugher everybody just as much and Oata would maybe throw the drankahma at me.

So I walk first to Muttachi's, and for sure she is browned off.

"Yasch, you schuzzel! What the people will think! How can you such a thing do? Didn't I learn you nothing about bad and good? What do you think that girl is, a strong? And you a bull?" Muttachi is just coming the door out with the night pail so she can empty it in the beckhouse, and she is talking so hard that the white lid with the red rim falls off and bangs on the cement step. That makes it a little bit more easy, because when Muttachi is mad and shouting it is not so bad as when she is mad and doesn't say nothing. So I pick the lid up and put it back on the pail.

"Carry the night pail already away, before you spill it on yourself!" Muttachi tips the pail at me but I hop out of the way fast enough so nothing gets on Futtachi's suit.

Muttachi looks me on, then throws the whole pail, but it is empty now and rolls away into a puddle.

"Yasch." Her voice is still now. "That suit looks not so bad on you, you know. I heard some women say in the church that Yasch quite nice looks when he all dressed up is." Muttachi scratches herself under the arm and looks me down and up. "Do you think it will be good enough for the wedding if we go to the dry cleaners with it?" I wonder me how she is thinking.

"Who's having a wedding?" I say.

"You and Oata!"

90

"Me and Oata? Are you making gooseberry wine again?"

"Yeah sure. You and Oata. I mean you stayed by her place for night two times already."

"So what, I always stay for night when I work out some place."

"But this is different, to do it when...."

"What's so different?" I want to see if Muttachi will say it.

"Yasch, you must start to think about what you will do with yourself. If you marry yourself with Oata you will have a farm and then...."

"Muttachi! What are you thinking about? I'm finished with working by Nobah Naze Needarp! I still work with Ha Ha Nickel and I just came to put on some...."

"Ha Ha phoned!"

"What!"

"Ha Ha phoned on the farmer phone. He said to me that he doesn't need you to work out no more and that you should come and get your truck." Muttachi goes to pick the night pail from the puddle. I have to swallow some spit before I can talk.

"What you mean he doesn't need me no more? I have a job there till threshing is finished. That's what he said when he hired me on! You were with! You were with when we hooked on there after we were by Knibble Thiessen when your back was to nothing! You heard it when he said he needed me from saddle time till after threshing! And if he got the egg contract he would have work all the winter through! You were with! You heard it!"

"I tried to tell it to him when he phoned today before I even stood up but he said he doesn't need you no more. So, what can you do? If he doesn't want you, you can't work there. And he said you should get the truck, today." Muttachi picks up the night pail lid and goes to the well and starts to pump water over it.

What the dukkat is happening here? Ha Ha Nickel doesn't need me no more and Muttachi tells me to marry with Oata and get the farm. I mean sure I was thinking how to get Oata's farm, too. But when somebody else tells you your own thinking it doesn't seem like such a sweet idea. And how will I play catch with Sadie if I don't work out there? And I feel again like a tumbling weed that the wind just rolls over the field any old way.

Muttachi carries the empty night pail into the house and I go after her and sit on the bench behind the table. I feel suddenly hungry and it falls me by that I didn't eat nothing since before Nobah Naze's funeral yesterday.

"I made some hova grits. You will like that, huh? Just like you had by Nobah Naze last year." Muttachi puts a bowl down and shoves in some porridge from the pot. At least Muttachi doesn't put in so much salt like Oata always did. But when you have it sometimes three times a day and it's haying time, you get used to it, a little.

After I eat I go up to my little room under the rafters and take off the black suit. I start to put on some field clothes, but I stop and I lie myself down on the bed. I wonder what Sadie is doing now that the school is finished, and I think she is maybe on the tractor or the hayrack with just her blue jeans that are cut off and her black brassiere. And I want to be close to those thin brown legs. And I wonder what Pug Peters did with her when he took her to the "Town Without Pity" show. I wonder if he would try anything. I mean she is just only fifteen. Then I fall to sleep a little bit and Muttachi calls me for dinner and I sit on the bed and I wonder if Oata got the cows milked and if she fed the pigs, too. And I wonder what she is eating for dinner and if she has some more chokecherry wine in the cellar.

Muttachi calls me again and I put some clothes on and go down. She doesn't say nothing for a while, she just eats. Then she says, very still, "You must marry yourself with Oata before it too late is." I don't say nothing back, I just eat. "I mean, not tomorrow, but soon, after Nobah Naze has gotten comfortable in his grave. That should be soon enough. You know Yasch, this is your big chance."

92

"Oh Muttachi! Be still! You talk crazy!" I am getting with all this already mad.

After dinner I go outside, gribbling out what to do. And it seems like I have to walk to Ha Ha Nickel's. At least if I have my truck I can go someplace. If I have some gas. And Ha Ha has to pay me something yet, too.

So I start to walk the road along to Ha Ha's place, about two miles. It is warm now after the rain and the grass in the ditch will be soon high enough to make hay. When I have walked almost a mile I see something drive out from Ha Ha's yard and turn this way. Then I see that it's my half-ton. It speeds up quite fast then it skids in the loose gravel and stops me beside. Sadie is driving it and she has the radio on loud to CKY.

"Hey Yasch," she yells. "You want along? Then creep right in." She laughers herself. I look both ways down the road. Nobody is coming. I open the door on the woman's side and sit on the piece of plyboard I have there so the springs can't poke you in the narsch. Sadie is wearing her jeans that are cut off and she doesn't have a blouse on. Just one of those things that covers the front and is tied up in the back. She is barefoot, too, and I wonder if she can hurt her foot because there is no rubber on the clutch.

I make the door closed and Sadie revs the motor and pops the clutch and the tires spin in the loose gravel. She laughs, steps on the brake and the truck slides to a stop again.

"Dad said if you didn't come to get the truck by dinner time I should bring it to you. He and Mom went to Winnipeg early in the morning." She pops the clutch again, and the truck swerves a little bit in the loose gravel. She doesn't stop this time. "Hey, this truck is fun to drive. How come you never let me drive it before?" She has it already up to sixty on the loose gravel. Then she slows it down and turns onto a field road and steps on it again. I don't say nothing, just watch Sadie and the road. I can almost see behind her top when she hunches herself down and I can't help myself, I have to look.

93

She is almost going sixty again when I see the harrow section in the middle of the track and so I slide over into her and grab the steer, too, and I swing it around hard so the truck drives into the flax field on the driver's side and then I swing it back onto the road again. Sadie's foot is off the footfeed now and the truck slows down and then it stalls because she doesn't put the clutch in. The half-ton stops and I am almost sitting on Sadie's lap. I move over a little bit, then take her by the shoulders. Her face is real white.

"You okay?" I say. She looks me on a little funny, then she shrugs herself out from my hands and says, "You can drive now. Your truck's no good!" Then she laughs and climbs over me with those long bony legs and sits on the plyboard on the woman's side.

I slide myself behind the steer, back up a little, then I climb out and throw the harrow section off the road. When I get back in the cab Sadie is sitting with her back against the woman's door and her feet on the seat. It's nice to have a seat full of legs.

'Well," I say. "Where shall we go?"

"Got a girlfriend now, huh?" Sadie pokes me with her toe. My face gets red, but I don't say nothing. "You like the big ones, huh?" Her whole foot is on my ribs. "Nice and soft, huh?" My hand grabs her ankle and I reach for the other one and pull her on to my lap. "Yasch stop! Don't! You bugger!" I lock her between my arms, and rub her cheek with the stubble on my face. I can feel her heart clappering against my ribs. And her shoulder bones through my hands. Then I see again the ditch I'm in. If I let her go she will laugher herself over me; if I do something more there will trouble be. How can I say to her how much I like her and what my dreams are? I am the hired man, just. Who got fired. And she is just fifteen, and likes to tease. And I am angry. I squeeze her tighter, then say in her ear, "How come your old man doesn't want me to work for him no more?" She stiffens herself and tries to wriggle away. But I don't let her, and then she goes soft. I hold her so she has to look me in the eyes. "What was loose?" I say. "I thought there was lots of stuff to do."

"I don't know!"

"Sure you know!"

"Promise to let me go if I tell?"

I give her a tight squeeze then I let her go. She quickly slips from off my lap and she sits close by the door. She doesn't put her feet on the seat now. I wait.

"Dad doesn't like the way you were looking at me all the time."

"What do you mean? How was I looking at you? Does looking hurt?"

"Mom didn't like that I was going to ball games with you all the time."

"But they never said you couldn't go!"

"And Dad said that the way you were looking at me all the time you might try something yet."

I don't know what to think. I didn't do nothing.

"They said you were too old and such a dow-nix, too."

"A dow-nix? I'm a dow-nix? Didn't I *work* for your old man? Do you think I'm a dow-nix?"

"No."

"Do you like the way I look at you?"

"Sometimes."

"Do you think I will try something with you?"

"I don't know."

"I'm a dow-nix but it's okay if you go around with Pug Peters. Does your old man know that Pug Peters lets the calf suck him off? Does he know that?"

Sadie says nothing. I stay still, too. And then I start to feel silly. I mean I'm twenty-three years old and I get myself all mixed up over somebody that's fifteen only.

"Sadie," I say so low that I can hardly hear it myself. And I feel my face getting real red because what I will say is like I'm

95

going to tear something out of my insides, but maybe it's better if I tear it out. But then I can't say it. When you say something like that you maybe tear the person you say it to, too. And too much I like Sadie for that.

I look at Sadie, look into her eyes. Then I give her a smile. She smiles back a little and I think I see a little bit from the old Sadie come into her eyes. I hurry and start the truck because soon she will tease me again.

I drive slowly to Ha Ha's yard. When we are almost there I see that she has her feet again on the seat. When I stop in front by the house, she pokes me again in the ribs with her toe.

"Yasch?"

"Yeah?"

"Is it true what you said about Pug?"

My baseball glove is lying on the floor of the cab. I reach down and pick it up. I give it to her. "Here," I say. "It's for you. We played some good catch together."

"Aren't you going to tell me?"

"You're too good for him."

"C'mon tell me."

"Ask him."

"Ah shit, you liar." And Sadie jumps out from the cab and runs into the house with my baseball glove.

So I drive to the parlor and haul out a twelve. And I feel a little bit good that I gave Sadie my baseball glove. And the first beer tastes good as I drive the middle roads along. But the second one is a little bitter and the feeling tears at me again. It's not so easy to get over it. And I get mad again that Ha Ha fired me because he thought I would try something with Sadie and I start to think that it's all because my Futtachi never much land had and we never had much money and we lived on the wrong side of the double dike and then my Futtachi went to Mexico and didn't come back and I feel like clawing out like my Futtachi did but then I think about what that Mexican in the

Neche pub told me that time how Futtachi had died with a knife in his back because he gave a Spanish girl a ride in his car and I open another beer bottle and I think about Sadie jumping for my pitches like a willow in the wind and I wish I could claw out some place. And I think how stupid it is in this world when you get in trouble because you feel things and it shows through and people get scared from you because they think you will do them something.

I look down at the eight bottles still left in the case and it seems like drinking beer all by yourself is like going to the ball field when the game is over and I come to the spill way that leads to the double dike and I turn on to the dike and drive it along with another beer in my hand. Soon I am close to Oata's place and I stop there on the dike and look at Nobah Naze's fields that I last week just finished seeding. And I wonder me if Oata is still mad with me and what she is doing. Why she should be mad with me I don't know for sure, because she was always after me last year when I worked out for Nobah Naze, and I was always trying from her to get away. And when she had on that pink dress when her Futtachi was in the hospital *she* went in the cellar and got the catsup bottle with chokecherry wine and *she* led me on so I didn't do nothing she didn't want me to do. And then she sure nutzed me out while getting the funeral ready. And she made me take her from the funeral home and stay with her in her bed. And then she throws the tubdewk at me in the morning. And I thought it would be so easy, that a fat woman like Oata would take anything she can get. And I would get the land.

I drink another beer and try to think what to do. And then it seems it's like learning yourself to throw a curve ball. You have to try again and again, hundreds of times, and then all of a sudden you get it. Never say die. So I drive to Oata's, finishing the beer bottle while I drive. It is about milking time when I get to the yard. I don't see her. I go close to the barn and listen. At first I don't hear nothing, then I hear the shtrulling sound of milk going into the pail. Good, I think, and I go around by the back of the barn to the water trough and I see that it is empty. Now Nobah Naze's farm doesn't have a waterhole so you have to pump all the water from the well. And Nobah Naze was always too cheap to put in a motor pump so it means pumping by hand. And in the summer time the cows drink lots. So I start to pump full the trough. Up and down with the handle. When I have the trough about half full I all of a sudden have to drain my radiator real quick and I hurry beside the barn and water the mousetail that is growing there. I hear something up behind me but before I can turn to look something wet hits me on the head and runs down my shoulders. It is warm and sticky and white. I turn to look and there is Oata standing in the hayloft door throwing the milk pail. I duck and it misses but it splashes into a fresh cow pie that splatters full my leg.

"Go already away you mustard boar!"

"What's loose with you now?" She throws a pitchfork at me and I hurry myself back to the pump. She goes away from the hayloft door and I pump water till the trough is full. The two cows come out of the barn but I don't see Oata. I go in and she is cleaning the gutter with a four-tined fork.

"I thought I said you should go away!" She has a forkfull of manure and she holds it like she will throw it at me.

"I just came to see if I could help you."

"Go help Ha Ha Nickel!"

"I don't work by him no more." Then I say, "He fired me."

"Fartzing around with Sadie, huh?" I get a little red.

"No," I say. "He just doesn't need me no more." Oata puts the manure on the wheelbarrow and picks up another load. "Here, give me the fork."

"No, I can do it myself!" She holds the fork in front of her and when I take a step closer she holds it higher. "And you're drunk, too. The last thing I need around here is a zoop zack! Go away!"

"Did you feed the pigs yet?" She lets the fork down and looks me on funny. Quickly, I grab the fork handle but she doesn't let go and the manure spills on my shoes and then she slips and we both fall down over the wheelbarrow and the manure tips over us.

"Yasch, you dow-nix! Look what you've done! I'm all full of mist!" Then all at once she starts to laugh and she laughs and laughs and laughs. And I start to laugh, too. Then I sing, "In the misty moonlight" and she laughs so hard that I think she will come apart.

But such a laugh doesn't away the problem take. Sure, she lets me help with the chores but then she sends me away, and doesn't even let me wash the manure from my hands. But I say a nice "Good Night" to her, and drive to Hauns Jaunses' Fraunz's waterhole and wash myself off and my clothes, too, and so I am all wet when I come home and Muttachi wants to know what is loose and I say to her that I asked Oata to marry with me and she pushed me in the water trough. Then Muttachi smells the beer and the manure on me and she gives me one on the narsch with the flyclapper.

Anyways in the morning I stand up early and drive to Oata's place and do the chores. Oata isn't up yet, but I do everything I can, then I go to the house and get the milking pails. Oata has the screen door hooked so I knock on it but she doesn't come so I find a piece of wire and I stick it between the door and the frame and lift the hook out from the eye and get the pails from the kitchen. Then I go milk the cows. I don't like to milk cows and at home I always let Muttachi do it, but I do it now and I sing Hank Williams while I squeeze the squirts of milk in the pail. But Oata's cows don't like the way I milk too much and they keep slapping me with the tail, but then I get the right beat that fits the song and the milking and it goes okay and I even get a good froth on the milk. I get a good pail from each cow and I carry it back to the house. Oata still isn't to be seen so I put the cream separator together and start to creamer the milk. Nobah Naze's separator is better than Muttachi's and I sing along with the pouring of the milk and the cream into the pail and the anti-freeze can.

Still Oata isn't anywhere and I don't know where to put the milk and the cream. So I set it on the table and I go on tip toes up the stairs. Oata is lying on her bed snoring like a Model T and one foot is sticking out from the blanket. A feather is coming out from the pillow close to her ear so I sneak it and tickle her on the foot. First nothing happens, then I do it again, and she kicks her leg so that the blanket is off all the way to her knee. Now I tickle her leg up to her knee and she kicks herself up and slaps her knee with her hand like there was a mosquito there. Then she sees me.

"Yasch! You hund! What are you doing here?"

"It is almost dinner time. You should stand once already up!"

Oata looks at the clock that stands on the dresser and she sees it is only half-eight. She throws the pillow at me.

"What shall I do with the milk and the cream?" I want to know. She looks me on like I'm talking French or something.

"You mean you milked the cows?"

"The chickens too but the boar wouldn't let me."

Oata hangs her legs over the side of the bed and she sticks her fists in her eyes and she yawns. "I'll put the milk away," she says. I just look at her a little bit, look at those rolls of fat under the nightdress. "Well, go then already. Can't a person put on her clothes yet without a dow-nix mustard boar looking her on?" And she picks up a pin cushion that is full with needles, throws it and hits me on the shoulder. I hurry go the stairs down and I think maybe Oata could play baseball good if I give her a chance. Then I remember that I gave my glove to Sadie. I start to feel hungry but Oata isn't calling me for breakfast so I figure I must go back to Muttachi's to eat.

For sure Muttachi wants to know where I was because she can't think of ever a time when I stood up before she did and I

100

just say, "I was making a land deal." And she looks me on like she is a little bit happy for me, then she looks me on crooked and I know she has her head in the beckhouse. It's bad when your own Muttachi can't think about you nothing good.

After breakfast I change the oil in my truck and I fix up the plyboard on the woman's side of the seat so that it won't slip around so easy and I even get a blanket to put over it. Then I look over the field and I see Zoop Zack Friesen is cutting the grass on his section of the double dike and I figure maybe I should go back to Nobah Naze's to see if I can make his grass machine ready. When I let the truck loose Muttachi comes running from the garden with the hoe.

"Yasch, where you going to?"

"Make hay when the sun shines," I say and I spin off.

When I get to Oata's there is a big blue Oldsmobile parked by the house and I don't know whose it is. But I figure I'll know soon enough and so I go to the grass machine and look it over. Nobah Naze's grass machine is still one of those olden ones that has a seat and somebody has to sit on it to lift the blade up and down. Well, I figure Oata could sit on the grass machine last year, so she can do it again this year. But I know that the blades have to be sharpened. Last summer the knives couldn't hardly cut nothing but Nobah Naze wouldn't sharpen them because he said he would new ones buy for this year. Well, he didn't. So I start working with the file until I hear the Oldsmobile let loose. I hurry out and see a man drive away, and Oata is standing on the step with her pink dress on.

"Who's the fancy dude?" I say.

"Wouldn't *you* like to know?" she says. "What are you doing here anyway? I thought I told you to go away."

"Fixing the grass machine up," I say. "But I guess I'll have to paint it pink, too, before you will sit on it. Or maybe you can take that tent off."

"How come you're fixing the grass machine?"

"What am I supposed to cut the hay with, tin scissors?"

She doesn't say nothing to that, she just scratches the cement step with her pointy-toed pink shoe.

"That was the lawyer with Futtachi's will," she says.

"So what did he say?"

"That kammers you nothing." And she goes into the house.

So I go back into the shed and sharpen some more knives and if you work steady it doesn't take so long. When I go back outside to put the blade back in the grass machine Oata comes outside again and she has the pink dress taken off and she looks like she wants to work.

So we cut the hay that day and the next, Oata sitting on the grass machine and me on the Ford tractor and it goes okay, even when it sometimes feels like it will all tip over when we cut along the steep parts of the dike.

A few days later we rake it with Nobah Naze's old horse rake and again Oata sits behind on the rake. Another few days and Oata calls up Baler Bergen and he bales the hay and me and Oata get it into the loft all dry. But Oata doesn't ask me for supper or chokecherry wine and when I get close to her I have to watch out for her elbows or sometimes a falling bale. I tease her a little bit but most of the time I try to be real nice. Once I ask her again what the lawyer said about Nobah Naze's will but she just says, "Chew your own cabbage!"

Then, when the hay is finished, I cultivate the summerfallow with that old blue Fordson Major but that sure is no 4010 John Deere. Still, the job gets done, and Oata brings me faspa on the field that day but she doesn't have her blouse flying open this time and she doesn't come with the Ford tractor neither. She comes with *my* truck. I am a little bit bedutzed about that. That could mean something.

"Who said you could my truck drive?"

"What's loose with you? You think only skinny Nickel can a half-ton drive?"

Now what knows she about that? And then it falls me by that maybe she jealous is. So I try to take her around with my arms when she is taking the faspa out of the cab and I get a chokecherry syrup bun in the face.

Then Ha Ha Nickel sets it all up for me. He phones on the farmer phone one day while I'm eating supper and wants to know if I will to Winnipeg drive with his half-ton and pick up for him his new Honey Wagon. I say sure, and he tells me to come by in the morning. I hurry drive to Oata's and ask her if she wants to go with. She doesn't say nothing to nerk me, she just says sure.

So in the morning I put on the best clothes that I have except for Futtachi's black suit, shave myself good and even smear on some green shaving lotion that I bought from the Rawleigh man one time and I drive to Ha Ha's to get the truck. Ha Ha is eating breakfast when I come and he says come in and have coffee so I do. Sadie comes from up the stairs and she has just her night dress on and she sits down by the table, too, and I only look her on a little bit and she makes a face at me. Ha Ha goes to his desk where he all his papers keeps and he gives me the bill that I have to give to the Honey Wagon people in Winnipeg. Then he gives me my pay, too, from when I still worked with him. He doesn't say nothing about why he fired me and I don't ask.

"Are you taking Oata with?" Sadie is sitting with one foot on the chair and she has her hands gripped around the knee.

"Chinga freow met sukka bestreit," I say and hurry go outside because I feel like I must to the beckhouse go.

Oata is ready when I come and she has the pink dress on again and it looks quite nice when she stands there on the step. And it is good to drive a new half-ton with a radio that's clear. The sun shines warm and bright when we drive the Post Road along to Emerson and then on the pavement the truck rides so smooth and the radio so clear is that I reach over and put my hand on Oata's knee and she doesn't even hit me with her pink purse.

And I drive the speed limit just because it is Ha Ha's truck and I don't want the wind to blow up Oata's dress too much and we look at the fields and the trees that grow along the river and the towns where the highway goes around and the States cars that go us fast for-by. And then when we get to Morris Oata says that she was too excited to eat breakfast but she is hungry now so we stop by the cafe there and have bacon and eggs with toast, and the jam comes in those little squares that you have to lift the top off and there is only just enough jam to put a little bit on one corner of the toast.

And we see signs for the Stampede and Oata says maybe we should go there next week because Nobah Naze would never let her go to such things, and I say "Sure." And then we drive farther past those French towns and the CKY towers and Oata says it's almost like driving to Altona and we laugher ourselves good over that. And when we get to Glenlea there is a sign there for Hudson Bay blankets and there is a woman and a man on the sign that have white coats on with red and green stripes around the bottom and I ask Oata if she would like such a coat and she says no the stripes wouldn't be long enough to go her around. And we laugh good again. And Oata rutches herself over to the middle of the seat and leans herself on me a little.

Then we get already to Winnipeg and the road is wider and there are lots of cars and women with shorts on bicycles and there is a lot to watch out for but I let Oata lean on me even if my arm is a little bit getting tired. And I find the Honey Wagon place easy enough because Ha Ha made a little map on a calendar page to show me where to drive. So I drive in there by the Honey Wagon place and I see a sign that says 'Shipping' just like Ha Ha said.

I go in by this door with the bill and I see a guy with a yellow hat driving this funny tractor that has two forks sticking out in the front. So I wave my arm at him and he stops and I show him the paper and say that I want to pick up Ha Ha

Nickel's Honey Wagon. And the guy doesn't even say nothing, just points to a sign that says OFFICE. So I go in the office door and the first thing I see is this girl that sits by a desk and she has real red lips and fingernails that are long and red like a cat that stepped in a pail of red paint, and she is smoking a long cigarette. Her long thin legs are crossed and her skirt so short is that I think I will see Kingdom Come. She blows some thin smoke at me but doesn't say nothing. So I say, "I want to pick up Ha Ha Nickel's Honey Wagon." And I reach her the bill that Ha Ha gave me.

She takes the bill and stands up and when she turns from me away so tight her skirt is that I can see both the loaves from her hind end. She wiggles to a door that says MANAGER and I hear her say something, then she and a man laugh a little bit and she comes back and a little guy about five feet high comes out and he says, "Follow me."

So I go after him through the building and I see where they are making the new Honey Wagons and I hope they finished already making Ha Ha's. Then we go outside where they have lots of new Honey Wagons standing in a row and he looks at Ha Ha's paper and he looks at the numbers painted on the side of the tank and then he says, "This is the one." And he tells me that I can just back the truck up and hitch it on and drive away. Back at the truck there is a guy from Gnadenthal that I baseball played against once and he is talking to Oata and he says when I come up, "Are you on your Honey Wagon trip?" and I say, "Yeah sure," and Oata is laughing when I get in the cab.

"Where want you to now?" I ask Oata.

"Winnipeg in the cellar."

I know she means to Eaton's and so we drive through all the cars with the yellow Honey Wagon behind and I drive real slow because I don't want to hook anything on and I don't want to drive any red lights through. So cars are honking us behind and it's almost like a wedding they so much noise make but I just drive slow because I know the way. I was here last year once. And we get there, too. But the guy in that parking place where you can drive your car upstairs doesn't like it when I want to park the Honey Wagon in there, but I show him that the tank isn't so high that it will hook on the roof and so he lets me through because there are already twenty cars honking after us. But the parking place is real full and we have to drive all the way up the roof before we can find enough room.

Oata is hungry now already and my stomach is hanging crooked, too, so after we go through the tunnel that is way up over the street we look in Eaton's for a place to eat. Oata sees it first, the sign 'Grill Room' and so we go in there and sit by one of those white tables. Some books with leather covers say what you can eat there and Oata says that she wants to try some of this French stuff and when she shows me where it says 'Filet Mignon' I almost fuhschluck myself because it will cost so much as two twenty-fours, but then I remember that Ha Ha gave me money so I say sure, and I snap my fingers like we always do in the Neche beer parlor and this old lady with a white paper crown on her head and red lipstick comes running over and I say, "Two fillet mig-nons please," and she writes with her little pencil on the little paper and she asks, "How do you want it done?" and I think a little bit and I say "Cooked" and Oata shakes her head up and down to show that she wants hers cooked, too. And the lady says "Soup or juice" and I say "Both" and Oata wants it like that, too, but when the lady says, "What kind of dressing on your salad?" I don't know what to say so I ask, "What kind you got?" She says "French, Italian, Thousand Islands, and Oil and Vinegar." So I say right away "French" because we will eat French food, but Oata says "Thousand Islands" and when the little old lady has gone away Oata says to me that she picked Thousand Islands because when she was twelve she found a pen pal once in the *Free Press Weekly Prairie Farmer* that was from Thousand Islands by Ontario and she would like to go visit there some time.

Well, the lady brings the soup and the juice first and we quickly drink the tomato juice because we are real thirsty already. Then we eat the soup and the lady has brought us some biscuits in little plastic bags, too, and Oata puts them in her pink purse so we can eat them if we get hungry in the store. The soup tastes pretty good, but the bowl is so small the spoon hardly fits in. Then the salad comes and my salad has this orange stuff poured on it and Oata's has some pinky stuff.

Then the Fillet Mig-non comes and all it is is some cow meat that isn't quite cooked because the blood still runs out and there is a big potato that is cooked with the peel on and then not even some gravy. But there is some butter so I smear it on the potato after I peel it and I say to Oata that at least they could the potatoes peel for us but she just smiles and I can see that she is happy for sure.

In Eaton's it is full with people, all women just, only some men, and you get almost dizzy trying to look them all on. Women with shorts on and red lips and toenails. Young thin girls with high heels and open toes and dresses that come only half to the knees or long dresses that they forgot to sew all the way up the sides so you can see the leg almost to the seat of knowledge. And one that we see when we go up the bale loader stairs has white pants on that are so tight and so thin that they look like they were painted on and you can see the red flowers on her underpants through the seat. And everyone has on lipstick, even old women like Muttachi. Then there aren't even enough live ones yet. They have all these big women dolls all over the place and some have nice clothes on, and some don't have any, and some just have legs and they are up side down and have double nylons on just. So many women a guy could go crazy in such a place.

But Oata has me by the hand and she pulls me from one thing to the other and we look at everything, and sometimes when we see something we know we say "Look, that you can buy in Harder's store" or "Such they have at the Co-ops" or "Fuchtich Froese had such a cap on the picnic." We go all the floors through and we laugher ourselves good at the place where they just have panties and brassieres, so many colors yet like a whole crayon box full, and there is one of those women dolls that has on just a brassiere and panties that are made from soft fuzzy feathers like baby chicks have. And Oata says, "That would tickle, not?" And I tickle her a little bit on the side and she doesn't hit me with her pink purse.

We go all the floors up even to the last one where they have beds and such but we don't buy nothing and we start to go down. Then we get to the cellar, where we didn't go before and it's different from the other parts. There isn't so much lipstick here and not so many shorts and red toenails. And no women dolls. Soon I hear people talking Flat German, and I look and I see some people from Gnadenthal, then by the shoes I see some from Winkler. By the soft ice cream and hot dog place, when we stop there for some, we see some people from Reinland and Rosengart and we talk them on a little while. It seems like half the cellar is talking Flat German. But then everybody goes to Winnipeg in the cellar.

But Oata keeps pulling me around like she is looking for something. Then all of a sudden she drags me over real fast to where there are Sunday suits for men.

"Yasch, you must yourself a new Sunday suit buy. How can you go to the church with me when you have on your Futtachi's old suit?" And before I can even swallow my spit to say something a man with gray hair who has his Sunday suit on and a yellow measuring string hanging his neck around comes and says, "Can I help you?" and Oata says, "He wants a Sunday suit to buy so he doesn't look like a schluhdenz when he to church goes." And the man says "Very well" and he takes me around the chest with the measuring string, and then around by my belt and he goes to a rack which is full with suits and he asks, "What color were you thinking of?" and I say "None" because that isn't a lie but Oata hurry says "Blue" and I can hear it from her voice that that isn't a lie. She has been thinking this out.

And before I can say anything more the storeman has hurried me into this little beckhouse to pull on these pants that are a foot too long and don't have any cuffs even, and next I am pulling on a Sunday jacket and then the man is sticking pins and drawing with chalk and he says to take it off and I can pick the suit up on Monday.

"But church is Sunday already!" Oata says. The man looks Oata a little funny on.

"Are you from the country?"

"Yes."

"I'll see what I can do," and he goes a door out with the suit.

"How come we can't take the suit now?" I want to know.

"The pants have to be fixed up."

"Muttachi could do it."

"You want to look like a schluhdenz like you did by the funeral?"

The man hurries back to us and says, "The earliest they can be ready will be tomorrow afternoon."

"That's good," Oata says. "Church isn't till Sunday. We'll come tomorrow." I start to go away but Oata pokes me and says, "Yasch, you have to pay yet." Oh, yeah sure. Will I enough money have? Then I remember that Ha Ha paid me so I have lots of money. But when I finish paying for the shirt and tie, too, over half my money is gone.

Well, driving the Honey Wagon in by the Eaton's parking place was easy, but going down is something else again. I mean to go down you have to drive through this curve tunnel that is so narrow and turns so sharp that in the first one I hook on the cement wall with the front corner of Ha Ha's new truck and the back corner of the new Honey Wagon tank. But I go real slow and make it through even if the city slicker cars are honking their horns behind. But then there are so many cars by the next level, and they won't let me get in the line and my foot is getting tired with holding the brake already and the cars are still honking behind. It is sure hot in the truck and Oata is getting tired with this waiting, too. So she climbs out from the cab and holds up a big Cadillac with her hands just like a police does. And the guy in the Cadillac holds his car still and I drive my rig past. Oata gets back in and we drive into the next curve tunnel and when the cars won't let us in the line again, Oata goes out and holds up a little Volkswagon and the lady that drives it holds still real fast because it looks like Oata might just push that little plaything out of the way just like that. So we get down to the street and the guy you have to pay money to wants me to pay double because he says I had two vehicles and I say to him that that isn't a vehicle it's a Honey Wagon and I give him half so much as he wants and drive away.

"Well, what will we do now?" I ask Oata when we hold still behind a red convertible that has a Lassie dog lying in the back seat.

"We have to find a place to stay for night."

"Stay for night?"

"Yeah, sure. We have to get your new suit tomorrow."

"But I have to bring Ha Ha's truck and Honey Wagon back."

"That's okay. Ha Ha doesn't need it so fast."

"But who will milk the cows?"

"I phoned to Hauns Jaunses' Fraunz and he said he would milk for me one day."

"Oh." I never knew that Oata could think so fast. "Do you know some place where you can stay for night? I have a second cousin that on Home Street lives, but he has an English wife and I don't know if he would let us stay for night."

"Yasch, don't be so dupsich. We will stay by a motel. What do you think those things are for?"

Yeah, sure. Now why didn't I think of that myself? That Oata, she sure has something behind the ears. Go to a motel for night. And I know where they are, too. On the road where you go home. For sure, staying with frindschoft would be like staying home and you have to say them everything about your Muttachi and what everybody is doing. Sure, a motel will be better.

The motel is nice. It has two big beds and rug on the floor and a little table with a lamp between the beds. There is a desk with a lamp, too, and phone and in the drawer is a Bible. And there is a TV, too. And a washroom with a sink and a flush toilet and a little bathtub with a shower on top. And there are some cups with paper wrapped around and there are lots of towels that say 'Voyageur'.

"Make the curtains closed," Oata says and when I go to the window I see a sign that says 'Beverage Room,' so I tell Oata that they have a beer parlor here and she says, "You go there then. I think I will a bath take." So I make the curtains closed and go to the parlor.

Loud music comes out the parlor door when I make it open and there is a line-up by the door and there is this big nigger with real big muscles in his arms standing by another door and he lets only two people in at once. But some people come out and I have to wait just ten minutes and it's my turn to go in. A young guy with pimples on his face yet and a white shirt leads me to a table where there are two girls sitting and they have long straight hair and white T-shirts and it looks like they don't have nothing on under because I can see two brown spots looking through by each one. They look me on once when I sit down but then they just talk some more like I wasn't even there and blow smoke to me. And they mix up their beer with tomato juice and they drink it and talk even if the band is playing such loud music it is hard even to hear myself when I tell the waiter that I want two glasses draft.

Then all of a sudden the loud music stops and some lights go on by the platform where the band is. Everybody in the room is still, except not the girls by my table. One of them is saying, "And then he pissed in the sink and she hit him on the head with the plunger!" But then the music starts again and a girl with a long night dress on it looks like climbs up on the platform and starts to dance with the music. And she wiggles her hind end a lot and lifts her dress to show her legs and once she opens the front wide real quick and we can see she has on something silver under there. Then when the song is almost over she lets the night dress fall to the floor and she has just on a silver strip on the top and on the bottom. Then another song starts and she dances some more and she turns around and bends over and her hands go back and it looks like she is taking the top part off but then she dances herself straight again and we can see that she another one on had under there only this one is smaller. And she is laughering herself. Then she starts to play with the silver on the bottom and she is bending her knees and she pulls the panties down a little and hurry pulls them up again and she does this a few times. Then just when the song is coming to the end she opens them up on one side and pulls them away from herself and there is only a very small piece of silver left there and it is tied on with silver string just. Then the next song starts and she turns herself around again and she bends herself over and you can't even the silver strings see and she is playing with her fingers on her loaves and then her fingers start to climb up her back and she is taking off what's left on the top and she throws it to the side and she turns around and there are two pink gopher tails or something hanging from each one and she starts to make one swing around like a windmill and then she starts to make the other one swing around only it goes the other way and she makes them go faster and faster until it looks like a two engine airplane when she spreads her arms out like wings and I almost think she will fly up.

Then the band holds still. The lights go out. And I hear one of those girls say, "How can she stand a guy like that?" And I wonder me if they didn't even look at the show.

I go back to the motel and figure Oata will laugher herself good when I tell her about the dancer and well you never can tell. But when I lock open the door and go in Oata is still in the washroom. All her pink clothes are hanging on the chair.

"Yasch, is that you?" Oata sounds a little bit scared.

"Yeah, sure. What is loose?"

"I can't stand up." I hurry go to the washroom door but she has it locked.

"The door is locked. How can I come in?" Oata is still and I look the doorknob over and I see there is a little button on the side and sure enough the door locks open.

Oata is all with soap sitting in that little bathtub. And for sure that tub is full.

"What is loose?" I say and I try not to laugher myself because Oata is trying to cover herself but there is too much.

"I'm stuck. I can't stand up."

"Oh. Have you been like this long?"

"Yes," she says, and I can see she has been crying. So I help her to stand up and tell her she should use the showerbath, then she doesn't have to sit down. I show her how to make the shower turn on and I pull the plastic curtain across and I go out in the other room and turn the TV on. I know for sure that Oata won't want to hear about the dancer right away.

So I look the TV on and it's news and you can see the man sitting a desk behind reading from pieces of paper and it's almost the same like radio except you can't do nothing else. You have to just listen and look.

Soon Oata says through the door, "Yasch, turn the lights out." So I do it but I leave the TV on and Oata opens the door a little bit and she says, "Turn the TV out too." Then it is almost dark and Oata hurries herself out from the washroom and under the blanket from the closest bed.

113

"You can switch the TV on again." And a different man is talking about the weather forecast and he has a blackboard with a map and he points to different things with a stick and I smell Oata from under the blanket and it smells so nice and clean and soapy that I stand up and say I will have a showerbath, too.

When I come back out again I feel real clean, even if Oata had used up almost all of that little piece of soap there, but I figure she has lots more to wash than me. Oata still has the TV on and she is lying under the blanket with just her face showing and she is looking at the TV. But she has the blanket opened up a little on the other bed and she says, "There's lots of room for us with two beds," and I know where she wants me to sleep. So I climb into the other bed and it's nice to spread your legs in a nice clean wide bed. And a late movie starts on the TV and we look at it and sometimes laugh a little bit and sometimes say "Did you see that?" or "Which one do you think did it?" but most of the time we just watch. One time when this girl in a showerbath comes on and she drops her shampoo bottle all the time and it doesn't break, Oata says, "Can you switch the TV out? I have to use the washroom." But she hurries back and we don't miss anything about the show.

It is almost half-two already when the movie over is and Oata is so still that I think she is sleeping already. But when I have switched the TV out and am lying in the bed again Oata moves herself around on the bed.

"Yasch."

"Yeah?"

"I like it that you are helping me with the farm."

"Nothing else to do."

"Is it so good as working by Ha Ha Nickel's?"

"Yeah…sure."

"I am real happy that you asked me with to Winnipeg."

I don't say nothing, just listen to a real loud siren going by on the road.

114

"You know, Yasch, I never went to Winnipeg without my father before and then we went just to the stockyards. Oh Yasch, I want to see so many things!"

The springs on Oata's bed boing and bong, so I shteepa myself up on my elbow and I see Oata sitting in the bed and the blanket is over one shoulder just and the yardlight is looking the curtain through and shining up her face and one breast. "Yasch, will you take me to see things?"

"Oh sure."

Oata throws the blanket off and swings her legs over the side of the bed.

"Will you take me to the Stampede?"

"For sure the Stampede."

"Oh Yasch, I am you so good. I am you so good." And then she is sinking on the edge of my bed and taking me around with her arms and holding me her breast against and pressing her chin down on my head. "Oh Yasch, you are me so good. You are me so good." And I wonder if she has any bones at all as she rocks me.

"Yasch."

"Yeah."

"We should get married." I don't say nothing but my heart is clappering real fast.

"Yasch?"

"Yeah?"

"Did you hear what I said?"

"Yeah."

"Don't you think so, too?" My heart feels like it is a fan that will fly off through the radiator.

"Yasch?"

"Yeah?"

"Well, what do you say?"

"Well…yeah sure…okay." I'm getting already dizzy.

"And you can buy me a ring tomorrow?"

115

"Yeah sure, I guess."

"Oh Yasch! I am you so good!"

And then Oata is climbing under my blanket and she is covering me with her acres and the crop is so big that I almost can't breathe and there is so much to disk and to plow and to seed and it seems like it will never be finished and the wild mustard keeps growing behind the plow and a cow bone gets stuck in the harrow and two crows are eating the seeds behind the drill....

Chapter Eight

So simple it isn't. Sure, I have hauled a few twenty-fours out from the parlor and before I go dead there's lots of chance that I will haul out some more. But I can affirm on a stack of Bibles that I never even sniffed a bottle cap that day. If I had, for sure I would have stayed home from church and people would say, "That Yasch Siemens sure is a dow-nix!" like always they have and they could have felt shtollt and fromm about it and it would still hail the same on the good man's field as on the bad man's and the rooster would still crow in the morning. And nobody would think that in the Gutenthal church the Devil had been.

Some things an honest man can't lie about. I mean, I tried. For Oata I really tried.

Engaging with Oata is a little bit like having the horse run away with the manure sled and you are holding the reins on and dragging the barnyard through just after the snow has melted in the spring. You hold on so tight as you can because you think it might be worse if you let go. You think you might never the horse again catch.

It was like I was dizzy then. I used what was left over from Ha Ha Nickel's pay to buy Oata the ring. Forty-seven cents in my trucker's wallet with the chain when we walked out from the wedding ring store, but that bothered me nothing then. I was thinking land. Seventy-nine dollars and ninety-nine cents was cheap for a half-section land. Oata was feeling like a queen, holding out her fingers so the sun would glance off the little stone in the ring that the storeman said was a diamond, except how would a person know for sure it wasn't just a rhinestone? All the way home from Winnipeg Oata held out her finger and she sat me beside humming with the radio along.

But the crop looks good on Nobah Naze Needarp's fields. Oata's land. My land almost. And I only think about Sadie Nickel maybe one time a day. Or two times. Or three.

It sure is different farming your own land. A person never has time to sit down except on a tractor or a milking stool. And you have to think about everything: spray the crops, get ready the swather, fix up the combine, patch the granaries, make ready the old auger motor that has the gas tank tied on with binder twine, ship the pigs, call Henry the bull to artificial the cows, sharpen the cultivator shares, last year's wheat to the elevator take, make chop, pump water, shovel manure, lend Zamp Pickle Peters's .22 to go hunting skunks under the granary, and worry when it doesn't for a long time rain. Then Oata says it's time to kill the roosters and I cut the heads off with the axe and by the time I've done ten I can do it with one hack and still have the neck in good shape because Oata the neck likes she says.

It is always already dark when fire evening comes. Oata calls me in from the barn or the tractor and she has the lights switched on, not the oil lamp. And she cooks real good now, not like when Nobah Naze still lived and was worried that the knecht would too much eat. But often I am so tired that I hardly eat nothing even when Oata reaches me more. Oata doesn't eat so much neither, at least not so much as I thought such a thick woman would, and she always tries to make herself look nice for supper. Sometimes she puts in her hair a little ribbon or she will smear on a little bit lipstick and she always on the table in a Blue Ribbon jar has some flowers. Sometimes Oata talks. Sometimes I talk. Sometimes we both don't say nothing and we listen to the clock or the radio. And then when it's time to go home I take her around with my arms and give her a kiss and try to schmooz with her but Oata only lets me a little, then wriggles herself away and says, "I must wash up the dishes yet." So I drive home where I have to always argue with Muttachi yet before I creep up to my bed under the rafters and fall asleep in my head with Sadie Nickel.

On Sunday mornings I hurry the chores and Oata has the blue Sunday suit ready and we drive to church in the '51 Ford. The people glutz us on there and fuschel and laugher themselves when we walk the church steps up so that it makes me feel like I forgot maybe my lowtz to zipper shut. Sunday after dinner I can have a nap if Oata doesn't want me to drive her to the mental home to see her mother which is every other Sunday. The other Sundays in the evening is the Sunday Night Christian Endeavor and Oata makes me to go to that, too.

Sometimes a thing will happen that wants to be forgotten and you think you have it erased from your head and then it comes back. Such a thing happened one time when I was young and it comes to me now, while I'm sitting Oata beside in the church. Maybe the singing is making it fall me by or maybe it's Forscha Friesen who is making the in-leading and he's standing up there so Christlich and everything or maybe it's Klaviera Klassen who is playing piano, I don't know. Maybe it's just that now when I'm engaged with Oata I have to all the time take her to church.

Futtachi had just moved us here from Yanzeed then, and I was in grade 4. Oata was in grade 1 just so I think she doesn't know. Forscha Friesen was one of the big boys in the school, grade 8, and Klaviera Klassen in grade 7, and she was his girlfriend supposed to be.

Forscha was like the boss in the school, only now it's hard to figure out why, because he used to play with plasticene and dinky toys on his desk and he was already fourteen. But he was the biggest and the others did what he wanted, even sometimes when they would have liked something different to do. You see, Forscha couldn't play baseball very good, and Penzel Panna once said to me that when Forscha in grade 6 was he played on the picnic right field and he missed a fly ball that he should have caught easy so the teacher took him out from the game and sent a girl to play for him. So now Forscha always tried to have no baseball playing at recess and dinner. The teacher didn't often play with us outside so his own way Forscha usually got.

Forscha's place was the first one around here to get television and so he always wanted to play cowboy like on TV. It was funny to see when I first to this school came and there was this big guy that pretended like he was Fury the horse and he would gallop the yard around and the other boys would gallop him after and even the girls sometimes. And two or three would be cowboys and they would the wild horse try to catch, but he was so big that he could break always loose. Sometimes he would bring his air rifle with to school and he had the lever made into a big ring and he would be the Rifleman and shoot all over the place. Or he would play Gunsmoke or Maverick or Have Gun Will Travel. Funny thing is he never had a cowboy hat.

When I to the school came they played Fury and they were all horses and they ran from me away into the bush and nerked me from behind the trees. This I couldn't figure out because in Yanzeed even the little kids baseball played all the time. But every recess and dinner they ran from me away for a whole week, and then I stopped them to chase. Why I chased them so long I don't know now except that when you are small you want with others to play and you do almost anything so you can.

But then Jesus came. And I wonder me now how Forscha Friesen can stand there behind the pulpit and talk about Jesus like there is nothing to it. I mean, I would think that such a thing would bother a person. But then it has sometimes fallen me by that maybe Forscha Friesen isn't a person at all. I don't know.

Maybe I should tell you something about this Sunday Night Christian Endeavor business. Really, nobody except the Christian Endeavor Committee calls it like that. Muttachi and the other old ones call it the *Jugendverein* (*Juide frei*, the young bengels call it) even when most of the Jugend only goes if they have to. Preacher Janzen likes to call it the Sunday Night service which maybe makes it sound a little bit higher in style so that Rape Rampel's daughter isn't embarrassed when she her English boyfriend home for the weekend brings. Anyways, the only time you hear about Sunday Night Christian Endeavor is at the end of the evening when you're so thirsty already that you think you can drink three dippers full of water and you are starting to feel so sleepy that you don't think you will to "Ask the Pastor" yet be able to listen when you get home and the Endeavor Committee leader stands up and reads off who will do the different things at the next service. Like who will be the chairman, who will say up a verse, who will a song sing, who will the children's story tell and such. Maybe the worst thing they can give a person to do is chairman because then you're supposed to pray yet.

So it's only the second time I'm at the Sunday evening church with Oata and my head is just swimming around because Sadie Nickel said up a verse and she was standing there in the front with a white blouse and a black skirt on that came just to the knees and her voice was so sweet that I couldn't even hear the words when Forscha Friesen stands up at the end and starts

121

to tell who will do the stuff next time. I'm already almost sleeping and don't listen to what Forscha is saying when all of a sudden I hear him say my name and at the same time I feel Oata's elbow in my ribs and then there is the sound of people trying not to laugher themselves. I can feel my ears getting hot and I don't even know what kind of soup I am in yet. So I bite my lip and stare at the waves in the wood from the church bench in front of me. A hand touches me on the shoulder and I jerk around and Forscha gives me a piece of paper on which 'Sunday Night Christian Endeavor' is written and the date two Sundays away and that Yasch Siemens is supposed to give a testimony!

Well, holem de gruel! It would have been easier to be chairman and just forget to say the prayer. Or if I wasn't engaged with Oata I could just not come then. But Oata will want me to do it, I think. I don't know why she wants to be so much in the church when the church never did much for her Futtachi and the people in choir practice laughered her away because she couldn't sing in the right gear. But I guess it's like me and the baseball team; you want something to be part of, and in a place like Gutenthal you don't have much choice of freedom there at all. Girls don't much play baseball here around so it's the church only for somebody like Oata. I mean, something Oata must know about what to people happens when they can't be part of things, because that's why her Muttachi in the mental home is. Only with me it's not the same. With the ball team I was part of something, but now I feel like I'm from the ball cut off.

His name wasn't really Jesus, it was Emmanuel Rempel and he came with his grandmother to live. He was in grade 6 and I could quickly see that a follower he wasn't. Right away I made with him friends and when recess came we played catch. "What's loose with him?" he wanted to know, when he saw Forscha galloping the yard around, and we laughed. Forscha galloped his herd of horses between us where we were playing catch and then took our ball from us away and threw it up on the school roof but it rolled down again. Emmanuel didn't say nothing when Forscha bothered us; he waited just till Forscha was away and he again started to play. The next recess some of the smaller ones that didn't have any fun with Forscha came and played with us, too. Then some girls came and we played scrub. Soon we hardly knew that Forscha in school was except when he would run through the baseball diamond and tear caps off and such.

This going to church business just makes me feel more cut off. And then to have to deal with Forscha Friesen yet. I see him standing there so shtollt and Christlich while the last prayer is prayed and when he thinks nobody is looking he turns his head and he looks me on with those light green eyes with dark centers and I can see that for sure he is the same Forscha that used to be boss in the school yard and that this testimony thing is his way to nerk me.

Then when I come the church out with Oata I see Pug Peters holding open the door from his car for Sadie Nickel. A minute later Pug's car tears the church yard out, gravel flies all over the place, and Ha Ha Nickel isn't even looking from where he is neighboring with Fuchtig Froese.

Oata doesn't say nothing about the testimony while I drive her home. I don't know what she thinks about it all. Only I think that if I don't do it Oata will feel bad. Oata asks me in for coffee, but I say no, that I'm tired and have to get early up to finish making the swather ready because soon it will be time to swath. So Oata gives me a little kiss and goes in the house. I slowly go to my half-ton and start to drive. I drive so slow that I don't even shift out from low gear, don't even switch on the radio, or the lights because it is still light enough that I the road can see. I just creep with the truck along hearing on the windshield the grasshoppers killing themselves.

A testimony? Sure I could gribble out what to say. I mean a person hears testimonies from young on. And I almost made one once by the weiner roast at Springstein camp. First you have to tell when you were saved, and if you can say for sure what day it happened that makes it even better. Like lots will say, "I was saved by the Brunk Tent Crusade in 1957," or "When Barry Moore came to Dominion City my boyfriend took me there and I was saved." Others say, "I was living in sin and then…" or "I was a carnal Christian" or "I was a backslider." So you can say how much has done for you the Lord and you say what your best Bible verse is like 1 Kings 21:21 or John 3:16, only you better say the right one because one time Porky Hamm was giving a testimony at Springstein camp and he said his best Bible verse was from Isaiah 53 and he starts to say "For God so loved the world" and we all laughered ourselves over him.

For sure, I could say something like that and it would almost be true. I mean, I could say, "I was living in sin till me and Hova Jake took Susch and Tusch from Sommerfeld to hear Wes Aram." I think the truest one would be the time when I was twelve years only and we were having every evening church for a week and Futtachi wouldn't let me with the other boys in the balcony sit. I had to sit him beside only three rows from the front. And the preacher preached a long time and then everybody had to kneel down and close their eyes and the preacher prayed and then he said that anybody that wanted others to pray for him he should lift up his hand and the preacher said "Pray for this old man here" and "Pray for this girl here" and I don't know but all of a sudden my hand lifted up and the preacher said "And a young boy needs your prayers" and then going the church out afterwards all those badels that were on the balcony were standing there on the church steps fuscheling "Pray for Yasch! Pray for Yasch!"

Sometimes we didn't play ball. Then Emmanuel would tell us things from Mexico where he lived before he came to us. And when he once started to talk you would just have to listen. His eyes would shine up and he talked like a song, it seemed like, and often Klaviera Klassen and the older girls would come, too. When the older girls were there we had enough to choose sides and play a real baseball game, or we would play Flying Dutchman or Last Couple Out. And if Forscha and his gang came to bother us Emmanuel wouldn't get mad, he would just wait till they were again away.

One day he brought some cards to school and he did some tricks like you had to pick a card and then put it back in the deck and he would shuffle the cards and tell you the top card to pick and it would be the one you picked the first time. Another day when the girls were skipping with their braided binder twine ropes he tied Klaviera's and Alma Martens's together. Then he made a lasso out of it and he started to twirl it around in the air. When the lasso was nice and big he twirled it over his head, then he let it fall down twirling all the time almost to his feet, then it twirled up again and over his head.

I drive on the double dike and when I am about a quarter mile along I hold still and switch off the motor and just look the window out. Then it falls me by that I still have some beer under the seat. So I start to drink a warm beer and look at it get dark. I feel really mixed up with Oata and the testimony and it burns me in my heart when I think about Pug Peters tearing out from the church yard with Sadie and that Ha Ha fired me because he thought I would do his daughter something and I schluks down the rest of the beer in the bottle and rip open another one that I have.

One morning I could see that Emmanuel had something in his jacket pocket but he didn't say nothing about it and he didn't show it to nobody. When the teacher the bell rang and we went inside I saw Emmanuel hurry put something in his desk. At recess I watched what he would do and sure enough he sneaked something his desk out and walked outside holding his hands in his jacket pockets. I hurried him after because I didn't want to miss nothing.

125

Emmanuel walked the yard across like he was really going someplace and all the small boys went him after. I think there were eleven and me, too. He liked it when we followed him so he led us the bases around. When we got to home base he stopped and signalled with his hands that we should between home base and the pitcher's base stand. So we did. Emmanuel reached his pocket in and slowly brought his fist out—and there he had a shiny red ball. He threw it up in the air with one hand and he catched it with his other one. This he did about three times and then all of a sudden he had a blue ball, too, and he was throwing two balls from one hand to the other and he went faster and faster, always a different ball to each hand, then he slowed a little bit and I saw his hand flitz into his pocket and then there was an orange ball hupsing in the air with the other two and he kept throwing them up and catching them and his hands so fast were moving it was hard them to see. And then all of a sudden he threw the orange one his head over and catched it his back behind, then the blue one, and the red one, too. This looked so curious that all the girls now were watching, and soon even Forscha and his herd were standing still by second base and looking. Then when everything was going the fastest Emmanuel catched the balls one after the other and it was finished. Klaviera hurried to Emmanuel and wanted to see the balls real close and Emmanuel let her hold them and she so excited was that she let one fall on the ground and she kneeled in front of Emmanuel to pick it up and then she held all the balls up to him and he took them slowly out of her hands.

Forscha scratched the ground with his shoe, then he made his horse noise, and he galloped Klaviera and Emmanuel between and knocked the balls to the ground. Melvin, Johnny, Schuzzel, and Abe came galloping right behind and they shoved Emmanuel out of the way and kicked the balls all over the place and then Forscha led his horses into the bush. Emmanuel didn't say nothing except "Thank you" when Klaviera gave him the balls again and he started to teach her how to do it.

And so went it then. Penzel, Jakie, Ronnie, Willie, Henry, and me would do what Emmanuel would lead us to do. And if the girls were there it was Klaviera, Alma, Judy, Emmie, and Trudy, only sometimes it seemed like Judy didn't like Emmanuel very much and that she wished that he would sometimes drop a ball and say bad words or something.

It is almost altogether dark when I see car lights turn on the dike and I see the red lights move away, then stop and go out. Somebody is holding the car still to shmuyng and that doesn't bloom the roses for me neither. So I drink out the beer and throw it over the cab into the ditch. Then I start the half-ton up and idle the dike along, the lights off, and just keep the wheels in the tracks that I can yet see because the grass so high is in the middle and in the summer time it never gets altogether dark even in the middle of the night. And I drive that car closer, I don't know why for sure or what I will see, only it's like something is making me go and I am a little bit scared about it just like, you know, when you have to go to the beckhouse more often than at other times. And then I can see the white that is the car in the black shadows and then I get close enough to see the shape of the tail lights and I know it is Pug Peters's white '54 Ford with the pink roof and I don't know for sure what I am doing only I don't stop. I just idle the truck frontwards till the bumpers touch and I give it a little gas and start to push the car and I turn the lights on but I can't see nobody in the car but I keep pushing and the car starts to shove off to the side of the dike a little and then I see a white shirt jump up and dive from the back seat to the steer and I switch my brights on and there I have Pug Peters's bare narsch bent over the back of the front seat wiggling forth and back while he is trying the car to steer so it won't in the ditch drive. I am laughing and mad at the same time and I give my truck more gas and push his car to thirty mile an hour and I want to push it right off the dike. Then I think that Sadie is in the car, too, and I slam the brakes on, shift in reverse and spin backwards as fast as I can. Then I turn the truck around and tear away down the double dike, laughing one minute and swearing a blue streak the next.

Then all of a sudden, when I'm off the dike already and only a mile from home, the motor sputters out and the truck jerks still. I know right away that I'm out of gas because I haven't filled with gas up after we brought Ha Ha's Honey Wagon back and he told Sadie to fill my tank full. And he gave me twenty dollars, too, but that didn't go far with putting money in the collect in church and buying Oata something to eat when we go to see her mother at the mental home. And it all of a sudden falls me by like a pie falling from a cow that I am flat broke, flatter even than last winter when my unemployment cheque was seventy-five cents just. I can't even buy enough gas to drive the rest of the way my truck home. I can't even buy myself a glass of beer if somebody gives me a ride to the beer parlor. Sure, I think, Oata will let me have some gas for the half-ton. I mean, I don't go no place except to work for Oata. And when we are married the farm will be mine, I mean ours. But what if it doesn't work that way? Oata won't tell me nothing about her father's will. Could I have done all this work for nothing? But Oata will give me gas and it'll all be okay. So I switch on the radio and reach under the seat and pull the beer case out and I find one full bottle in it yet and I bite it open and take a long warm skunky swallow. "Ask the Pastor" is on the radio and the people phone up and say "I have a problem" and it seems like the problems are all about people who live common law and some sound like they're drunk and others are just kids fooling around and some the pastor has to cut off because they are trying to swear at him but the pastor just keeps on with, "Hello, this is the pastor speaking," and the people keep saying, "Hello pastor? I have this problem, see," and I sit there in the dark truck sucking warm beer just listening to the pastor's voice and the women's voices on the phone, just the voices, not the words and then all of a sudden I hear a man's voice and it sure sounds like a voice I have heard before some place and I turn the radio louder and the man is telling his problem all about. And his problem is that he this fat girlfriend has who always is trying to make him do sinful things when they alone together are and she is so big and strong that he has to do what she wants. And the pastor wants to know why he doesn't stop going with her then and the man says, "But I lawve her!" and when I hear the way the guy says "lawve" I know it is Forscha Friesen!

Well, that for sure makes me mad! How come he so much knows about me and Oata? It's a good thing I have no gas or I would drive right over to Forscha's place and plow him one on the nose. But he's not worth walking five miles for. That's for damn sure. But I can't let him get away with this. For sure not!

One day lots of kids were away from school and some had to stay in by recess because they had laughed while we were saying the Lord's Prayer and so there was only Emmanuel, Klaviera, and Trudy outside with me by recess and we couldn't see Forscha any place. Emmanuel put his finger to his lips, then he signalled us that we should follow. So he led us the school behind and around the bush. When we had almost come to the end of the school yard he put his finger to his lips again and he got down and crawled some high grass through into the bush. Klaviera and Trudy crawled him after and I was last. Emmanuel still had his finger in front of his lips but it was hard to keep still. There, lying in this high grass so it's almost like a nest, was Forscha, and he had his pants open and his pisser was sticking out. And Melvin and Johnny were lying there, and they had theirs sticking out, too. All of a sudden Forscha said "Go!" and they all started to play with their pissers and it looked so funny that I was biting myself so I don't laugh but Trudy couldn't hold herself and right away those guys stopped and we four ran so fast as we could, all laughing. We got to the school just when the teacher was ringing the bell and we were in our seats already five minutes when Forscha and his horses came in. As soon as Klaviera and Trudy saw them they just started to laugh and they couldn't stop even when the teacher got real mad at them and even when they came to stand by his desk and he gave them each one on the hand with the strap. They couldn't stop and soon everybody in the school was laughing, even the teacher, but not Forscha and his bunch.

I finish drinking the beer bottle empty, turn the radio off, take the key out and walk the rest of the way home. Muttachi is leaning her head on the wall by the radio and "Ask the Pastor" is still on but she is snoring. I switch the radio off but I don't wake her up because I don't want to talk or to listen.

Sure in the morning Oata says I should fill my half-ton full with gas up, that I shouldn't be so bleed because the farm was for us together already even if we didn't stand the preacher in front yet and she starts to schmooz with me even if I didn't shave myself and we almost make fire evening before it's dinner time, but then I reckon I better make the swather ready because the sun is shining hot and the barley is ripe almost already. And I shame myself for thinking that maybe I was doing all this work for Oata for nothing and for sure a half-section land is better than Sadie Nickel and I only let myself think the land about.

That day after recess the younger ones like me were drawing pictures and the grade six, seven, and eights had to read out loud from the Bible. Judy was standing up and reading and all of a sudden she read something about Emmanuel and right away Forscha's hand reached up and he wanted to know what Emmanuel means. Everything was real still. The teacher coughed, and he looked that Bible page on and then he said, "It means Jesus. That was his name before he was born." Everyone was even stiller, and I saw that Emmanuel was looking straight in his Bible but his ears weren't red like mine would have been if I was him. Then the teacher said, "Okay, Schuzzel, now you read."

When school over was I heard Forscha say to Abe, "Jesus," and they both laughered themselves. Emmanuel was still when we were walking home at first but then he started to tell me about the snakes in Mexico and his voice just made me everything else in the world to forget.

For a while it was not so bad, just once in a while Forscha and his bunch would say "Here comes Yehsus" or when Emmanuel was juggling the colored balls those guys would sing "Jesus loves me this I know." And one time when Emmanuel was in the beckhouse they all stood around it and they sang, "Jesus puts his money in the Bank of Montreal—Jesus saves, Jesus saves, Jesus saves." Emmanuel just made like he didn't hear nothing.

The trouble with farming is that there is so much time to gribble. When you are shovelling manure or fixing the fence or driving the tractor your hands and your feet can do it all alone and your head can fly the world all over and you have to be careful that you don't gribble yourself into something you don't really want. Gribbling about the wrong thing could maybe make you lose your ball bearings. So I try not to gribble about the things that I am angst about. Though sometimes it is hard to tell what you should really think through.

I try to gribble only three things about. The land, for sure. I learn off by heart every puddle and ridge and I see where the crop is growing better and where not so good and I try to gribble out why. Then there's Oata who is so warm the last few days that every time she close comes I have to take her around with my arms and she presses me against and it's almost like her fat rolls just shape themselves to fit my knobby bones like thick syrup shapes itself to fit a crooked bottle. And a couple of times we almost don't stop ourselves, once in the garden behind the corn and once we almost laid ourselves down on the swather canvas after Oata brought me some tea with ice. And I know that one of these days I won't make it home for night.

But even yet I can feel Sadie and Pug and Forscha Friesen in the back of my head and sometimes when I alone am I get so mad that I feel like borrowing a .22.

I think too about the testimony even if I don't want to. And if I hold my head a certain way I can only see the good things from it. For sure Muttachi will be happy. And I think it will make Oata happy, too. That's the crazy thing about it. I mean, I think if I said to Oata that I couldn't do it she would understand. She would maybe even figure out something like going to the mental home to see her mother that day. But then Forscha Friesen would just put it on some other program. And if I don't do it it would mean that Forscha Friesen would be winning over me. That I can't let be.

Then I start to gribble out what this testimony business is all about. In my head I see how it was with other people that gave a testimony. For sure, they were all nervous. And when you watched them standing up there the pulpit behind saying something about themselves and sin and God, I don't know, it was like a person got a strange feeling, it's hard to say, something like one time when I was very small, maybe six or seven, and Muttachi took me with to visit these old people, and there were no children to play with, or some toys, and I was just sitting on a stool turning a button on my jacket and then the old man gave me a book to look at and it was a color picture book, a bit like comics, about the Bible and I paged it through and when I came to the stuff about Jesus I looked slowly and when I saw the pictures that showed Jesus on the cross with his clothes all ripped off, only a rag around the middle, it was like I couldn't stop staring at the picture. The picture wasn't scary, but the naked man on the cross with his orangy pink skin made it feel very warm there on the stool like if something was tickling you all over only not the laughering kind of tickling and that thing in the pants was too much there and it was hard to sit still on that stool.

I try not to gribble about it, it scares me to have such things in the head, but it's there, how it was sitting on the church bench looking at somebody standing in the front giving a testimony and it was almost like they were undressing for everybody to see.

Anyways, on Sundays after dinner we would always visit with each other and we would figure out in Sunday school already where we would together get. So this one Sunday we decided that we'd go to Jaunses' Fraunz's waterhole to swim. After dinner I hurried myself away from the table so Muttachi couldn't make me go with to visit some old people or some place where they just had girls and I ran to the middle road where we were going to meet. Soon Penzel and Jakie came with their girl's bikes and then Ronnie came walking with his slingshot. We stopped there and waited a little bit and Penzel let me ride his bike a little way and Ronnie almost shot a robin. Then Willie and Henry, who were in grade 3 just, came and they were each rolling a small tractor tire along and making motor noises with their lips. Slowly to the water hole we walked thinking that Emmanuel would soon catch with us up and before we knew it we were there.

It was quite a big water hole, but it was old and nobody used it any more because Jaunses' Fraunz was too lazy to have animals, so it was grown with willows around and had lots of grass on the waterhole hump. There were some thick boards on one end where you could go with a pail to dip water and so we went to stand on them and we threw stones at the frogs. Then Willie wanted to know what that was in the water there where the willows were growing out of the bank and hanging over the water. It looked like some wood but we couldn't see it all because the willows were hanging in the way and so we went around closer and we saw it was a rowboat half full with water. Penzel and me were the biggest so we took our Sunday shoes and pants off and went into the water by the boat. The boat was stuck in the mud a little bit but after Jakie found a rusty pail with just a little hole in it we shoveled as much water from out of the boat as we could and it came loose from the mud. There was one paddle in the boat and I found a long branch and then Penzel and me got in the boat and with lots of hard work we got it over to the thick boards where we let the other boys on. Water still leaked in the boat and Ronnie had to shovel it out with the pail, but slowly we moved the boat to the middle of the water hole. And Willie and Henry had some baling twine tied on some sticks and they fished and sang "I will make you fishers of men." Then we were in the middle and I poked down in the water with my stick and I couldn't touch the bottom with it.

"Hey look!" Penzel called and there we saw Emmanuel coming us towards on a thick board. He had just his underpants on and he was standing on this plank and pushing it to us with a long thin pole. Soon he was almost the boat beside and Penzel asked if he could get on the plank, too.

"Sure," Emmanuel said and Penzel stood up in the boat and started to climb over the side. Jakie and Ronnie stood up so they could see better and the boat rocked and Penzel flew in the water. His head came right away up and he screamed. Then he ducked under again. Nobody could swim, not even Emmanuel. Penzel came up again. Emmanuel shouted to him, "Hold on by the pole! Hold on by the pole!" Penzel woke up enough and grabbed the pole on that was poking in his face. Emmanuel pulled Penzel to the plank and then he told everybody to sit down in the boat except me and together we pulled Penzel out from the water and helped him climb into the boat. Emmanuel came into the boat, too, and with his long pole he soon had the boat by the side. Penzel was shivering, but it was a hot day and Emmanuel dried him off with his own Sunday shirt and made him warm. We lay there on the water hole side, then Emmanuel climbed all the way up to the top of the hump and the sun was shining him behind, right by his head, and it was quite something to see.

We didn't say nothing about this to nobody and we brought it by to the littlest ones that they weren't supposed to say nothing neither. Emmanuel acted like nothing happened and soon we didn't think much about it no more.

So it's going not so bad. I reckon out that the weighty thing for me is to keep my nose pointed the right way. That means the land and Oata. And to have the land and Oata I will have to live with the church along. Here around that's how it's done. So I tell it to myself that for sure it won't matter nothing what I say for a testimony as long as I go up there and say something. I mean, it's not like the people think Yasch Siemens is a preacher. If I just go up there the pulpit behind and stammer out something about how much the Lord has for me done and I say them a Bible verse won't they fuschel with each other, "Isn't that Yasch a good man now that he is with Oata engaged and goes with her to church?"

So I have it reckoned out. Oata is happy and Muttachi is happy and doesn't argue with me even when I don't come home for night one time. And on Sunday going to church doesn't seem so bad even if I have to look Forscha Friesen on but I don't let him see that he is bothering me one bit.

Then Monday morning I am going to Oata's when that blue Oldsmobile rushes me by on that long driveway and holds in front of the house still. A young guy in a Sunday suit creeps out. Soon Oata comes and he holds open the car door for her and she creeps in. Then that Oldsmobile almost drives me over when it rushes the driveway up again and it looks like Oata is waving to me only the car is going so fast that I don't know for sure. For sure it's crazy, but I am green! I know that guy is just a lawyer but what does he want with Oata again? How come she didn't say nothing to me that he was coming back? And then it comes me by again how come she won't tell me nothing at all about what the lawyer says to her. All she will say is that it kammers me nothing. Well, I figure it does kammer me something!

So I go into Oata's house and I pull open the drawer where I saw Oata take out Nobah Naze's permit book when I had to take the wheat to the elevator. I look everything through but there is nothing from the lawyer or about the will. Just a letter from the municipality that says that Nobah Naze Needarp didn't his taxes pay for three years already. I look all the other drawers through and then the piano bench yet, too, but there is nothing.

When I start to go upstairs the phone rings, and I don't know for sure if I should answer it, but when it has rang four times already I lift it up and it is Ha Ha Nickel.

"Uh, hullo Yasch. Is Oata there?"

"No." I am mad with him but he was once my boss and I try to talk steady.

"Did she go away?"

"Yeah," and then to make it sound important I say, "she went away with the lawyer."

"The lawyer? Which one is that?"

"The one with the Oldsmobile."

"Oh yeah. I know that one. Okay." And he hangs the phone up without saying even goodbye.

Well, what the shinda does Ha Ha Nickel want with Oata? And what kammers it him which lawyer it is and I start to think maybe I shouldn't have said nothing about the lawyer to him. And he sounded just a little bit different, not quite so sure with himself, and I wonder me if he knows that Sadie was schmausing on the back seat in Pug Peters's car. And I can see again that bare narsch in the brights from my half-ton and I am crazy with madness that I let Sadie Nickel get away and never tried nothing with her if she was going to let such a becksisheeta pull her pants down and then I wish that I had shoved that car right off the dike or pulled Pug Peters out of the car and made him stick it in the muffler or something and then it comes me in that Pug Peters and Forscha Friesen are cousins because Gnurpel Giesbrecht is both their grandfathers and ganz geviss I am feemaesich mad!

136

Then I hear honking outside and when I go out the door it is Hingst Heinrichs driving his Futtachi's new pickup with the big six.

"Schmuynging in the middle of the day, ha Yasch?" he laughers himself. I don't say nothing.

"Hey Yasch, you hear about Pug?"

"No, what did that schwengel do now?"

"That schuzzel is going to be a foda in about eight months!"

"What?"

"Yeah, that shaubelkopp has been riding the horse without a saddle and now Ha Ha Nickel is hurry making a wedding." Hingst is laughering himself so much that his Player's Plain falls from his lips.

I can only swear. Hingst finds his smoke and sets it back in his face.

"Yeah, that stupid Pug. I always told him he shouldn't measure the water in the ditch if he didn't have his gum boots on, but I guess some people don't have it all up there." Hingst cracks up again. "But he sure don't shoot blanks down there!"

Hingst spins his tires and stops again.

"They said at the store today that Ha Ha is trying to find a place for the young pair to live. Maybe he could pacht for them my sister's playhouse!"

Hingst yuckers himself like crazy again and he tears away down the driveway and I feel like I was driven over with a D-9 Cat.

"Yasch! Yasch! Stop it already!" Oata is pulling me on the belt and knocking me on the shoulder with her fist so I will let the Oldsmobile lawyer loose from where I have him by the collar bent the car hood over. "I will tell you everything. It's not his fault!" So I let him loose and back with Oata away. The lawyer uprights himself and makes his Sunday suit smooth with his hands.

"You don't have to tell him anything, Miss Needarp. But maybe it would be good if you did." Then he hurry drives away.

"Come, Yasch. Let's go in."

"Ha Ha Nickel phoned for you." I am sitting on the chair with the crack in it but I will just let it pinch now till I know something.

"Yeah, I know. He phoned to the lawyer, too."

"What did he want?" Oata is zippering her dress down and walking to the stairs.

"He wants to buy the farm." Oata is almost up the stairs already.

"But you won't sell your farm, will you?"

"Yasch," Oata is calling from upstairs now and it sounds like she is pulling her dress over her head. "It is not my land!"

"What you say?" I call back because I don't want to believe.

"This is not my land!"

"Not your land!"

"No."

"Whose is it then?"

"My mother's." Oata is coming down the stairs in her working dress.

"Your mother's?"

"Yeah, who else?"

"But your mother is...."

"Crazy?" Oata is opening the door to go outside.

"Nah, well...."

"Maybe she is, but...." The screen door slams shut and I hurry her after.

"But will she sell it?" I call after her as she closes the beckhouse door after herself.

"She can't sell it." Oata hooks the door from inside.

"How come not?"

"My father's will says the land can't be sold if my mother is in the mental home." I hear some newspaper tearing.

"What if your mother comes out?"

"Then if she sells the farm she must give me half the money."

"Oh."

"How come do you think Ha Ha Nickel would want to buy this farm all of a sudden?"

I hear Oata hooking open the beckhouse door and I hurry turn my back so she can't see my face right away.

"How come do you think?"

I dig my toe in beside the board that leads to the beckhouse.

"They say Ha Ha," and I have to swallow real hard, "Ha Ha is making a wedding."

"Oh." I feel Oata touch my arm. "You mean Sadie?"

"Yeah, her and Pug Peters." I turn my heel in the earth like I am killing a mouse that I stepped on.

"Sadie is so young yet. And with such a dow-nix, too."

I kick some fat hen that is growing there. Then I go sit down on the wooden bench beside the washbasin and I lean over with my face in my hands. Oata sits me beside and puts her hand on my shoulder and leans her arm on my back and it is warm where I'm shivering even if it a hot day is.

"You like Sadie very much, don't you?"

I don't know what to say. I mean I'm engaged with Oata and I shouldn't like nobody else.

"It hurts, huh?" I wonder me how come she knows so much and I start to shame myself because my eyes are getting wet.

"Yasch, did you listen to 'Ask the Pastor' last time after you brought me home from Jugendverein?" I open my eyes and look her on.

"Yeah."

"Did you hear Forscha Friesen?"

"You knew it was him, too?"

"Sure, that schaps I would any place know!" Oata is still. The fridge motor starts up in the house. "Do you think it is true what he said? That I make you to do sinful things?" She says it so fast that it feels like a whip. Like a piece of V-belt or extension cord. Like when Muttachi has caught you out for something and is spanking you but you know even when she is making your seat shring that she doesn't know the real bad thing you've done but the V-belt seems to know it. And all of a sudden you know that the real sin is between you and the V-belt and that if you ever told somebody about that the whole world would maybe fall apart. But I know something that I have to do and I take Oata by the shoulders and look in the brown eye and in the blue eye. And this time I don't wait for Oata to start something. I just give her the biggest and longest and suckingest kiss that Oata afterwards says sounded like a cow was pulling its foot out of the mud.

Forscha's gang started to nerk Emmanuel more and more. When they were drinking water they held a cupful to him and said, "Make me some wine from this." Or they called him "Baby Jesus." And after one time Forscha found Emmanuel sitting with Klaviera all alone behind the school he started to say worse things like "Jesus Murphy!" and "Jesus H. Christ!" Emmanuel just looked Forscha on like he was a grasshopper or something, then he walked away. But if Forscha's gang was close to us when we went home they called out loud things like "Holy Jeeze!" and "Christ Almighty!" and "In Jesus Name Amen!" Sometimes some of the girls laughered themselves a little, at least it seemed like Judy did, and one day I saw that she had written "I love Forscha" all over her spelling scribbler cover.

But it looked like Forscha thought that Klaviera still his girlfriend was and sometimes she would still walk the bush around with him if Emmanuel wasn't yet in school. Then one day she heard him say to Emmanuel, "Jesus Fuckin' Christ!" and she slapped Forscha on the mouth and told him he was a pig. The teacher came out with the bell just then and Forscha couldn't do her nothing.

Everything was quiet for almost a week. Then one day at recess when Forscha's gang was in the bush, Emmanuel called us together and told us a secret. We weren't supposed to tell nobody. We all shook our heads with him, even Judy, and it was such a secret that we didn't even say nothing to those that knew the secret, too.

Everybody comes to the Sunday Night Christian Endeavor, even those that have cabins by Mouse Lake. And it is such a hot Sunday that I can already feel the armpits on the blue Sunday suit getting wet and I only just put it on after I creeped out of the car with Oata at the church. But I have the Bible in my hand with the purple ribbon stuck in by the right page like Oata showed me. And the testimony that Oata helped me to write up is folded on a piece of paper inside. We walk in the church and it bothers me nothing that some people are still fuscheling and laughering after us. I know I can do it. For Oata I can do it.

So we sit together on the men's side of the church about in the middle and Oata takes my hand but it is so warm that she lets go because we are sweating so much we could easy be sitting in puddles soon if we don't let some wind us between. Lectric Loewen, the church father, goes around with his long hook and makes open all the windows he can but it helps nothing much.

Soon Klaviera Klassen starts to quietly the piano play and the people that are still neighboring on the church steps come in but they still neighbor some more after they sit down. The song finishes and Klaviera pages in her songbook, then starts to play "Do Lord, Oh Do Lord, Oh Do Remember Me" real soft and slow but then it seems the song grips her and she starts to play faster and louder and by the time she comes to the chorus the fourth time she is pounding so hard that it almost like thunder is and for sure nobody is neighboring any more!

But the piano thunders in my head even after Klaviera has stopped to play and Dola Dyck is already standing the pulpit behind and telling the people to page to a song and Oata takes the songbook out from the little feedrack that is on the church bench in front, but the piano still bangs "Do Lord" in my head

141

even after Klaviera starts to play Dola Dyck's song. And I have to bite my lips shut so I don't sing the wrong song. It's like Klaviera's song is trying to nerk me or something and I don't know what it is supposed to mean, but I can't make it go away. Not when the song is finished and Dola Dyck is saying the prayer with his eyes closed so tight. Not when Hingst Heinrichs's sister Kobbel says up a long verse. Or even when the quartet with only three singers is singing and Klaviera is playing again. The song just keeps thundering me in the head, not just the piano, but the words, too, only it's not the right words. It's like the song is saying "Do Yasch, Oh Do Yasch!" And I don't know what I will do, what I am supposed to do, I mean sometimes such things mean something like the farmer who was working in his field and he's driving his tractor along and he looks up in the sky and he sees in the clouds the letters P C and he wonders what it means and he gribbles about it all winter and reckons it means Progressive Conservative so when the vote is called he runs for the P C but the Social Credit wins and so he goes back to his farm and is plowing and again he sees P C in the sky and this time he prays about it and it comes him by that it means that he is supposed to preach Christ and so he learns himself to be a preacher and then he is happy.

Oata gives me one with her elbow and she fuschels in my ear that it is time for the testimony, so I grip my Bible on tight and stand up and start to walk to the front and then all of a sudden I am climbing the steps up to the platform and I am almost to the pulpit when I see the preacher that is supposed to talk after I give my testimony and we have sung a few more songs and Dola Dyck has said at least one more prayer. I know that I have seen that man someplace before but I don't know who it is, I just can't gribble it out. It just doesn't fall me by. The man looks me on and it is like he is smiling just a little bit with his eyes and it seems like this man has something to do with why I am going behind the pulpit. Then the man does something

142

strange. He waves to Dola Dyck and they go the platform off and sit in the benches. And I am alone.

I step behind the pulpit and put my Bible down on the slanted thing there and I reach my hand out for the nickel-colored microphone that looks like the front from a Massey-Harris 44 and I move it so that I can talk it in without bending over too much, just like the preachers do. Then I look at the church.

It sure is different looking at the church from behind the pulpit. The whole church full is looking you on. And you are higher than everybody. And everybody you can see. And it's almost like you can see what everybody is thinking, because you can see their faces. Oata is there, her face shining like the sun. Forscha Friesen is there, and he looks nervous, but he looks like he wants to laugher himself, too. Dola Dyck is there, sitting in the second row, but I can't find the preacher that was him with. I look the rows down. Ha Ha Nickel is sitting Pug Peters and Sadie beside. Zoop Zack Friesen, who usually to the free church goes. Hauns Jaunses' Fraunz. Schlax Wiebe. Knibble Thiessen, the rightmaker. Fuchtig Froese. Store Jansen's Willy. Yelttausch Yeeatze. Penzel Panna and his girlfriend from Altwiese. Rape Rampel. Milyoon Moates. Hingst Heinrichs. Gopher Goosen.

And on the women's side the women—Muttachi, her wet eyes glancing the light off like sparks—and the girls like Shtramel Stoesz and her sister Shups, that me and Hova Jake took to a crusade in Dominion City once. And the children in the front bench, waiting. And I see Klaviera Klassen sitting sideways on her piano bench and she is looking me on with such eyes that I have to look away and I see the boys in the balcony, all looking down to me and nobody is fartzing around like the boys in the balcony usually like to do and I see the preacher again on the balcony but he is just a boy now and he is looking at me waiting, his hand in his jacket pocket.

143

Then I start to testify. And when I hear my shtimm going through the loudspeakers it makes me feel hartsoft good. It makes me feel strong like a giant or Samson. And the heat bulb from in the ceiling burns down on the Bible. But I don't even look it on. I don't even open it to the ribbon page where on some paper my testimony is written down. I just tell the story and everybody listens. I tell it in Flat German. I tell it in English. I even tell some of it in High German. But mostly it is die gute language all mixed up.

And nobody moves. Nobody scratches themselves behind the ear. No men put their elbows on their knees and lean their faces in their hands and go to sleep. No child goes back to sit with their mother before the story is over. No baby cries.

And I feel my blue Sunday suit soaking in the armpits. I feel some sweat leak down my ribs. My tie is schneering my throat. But my throat doesn't get dry. And I tell my story to the front rows. I tell it to the back. I tell it to the men's side. And I tell it to the women. I tell it to the balcony. And that boy has a red ball in his hand. I tell it to the piano bench and Klaviera who is pinching it. And I tell it to Forscha Friesen who is chewing on the end of his tie.

My head feels like it's burning. My tongue is a flame. The boy is throwing his ball in the air. And the people don't look me in the face no more, they are looking at the top of my head. There are two balls juggling in the balcony.

My testimony can't be held up. I must finish it. Or burn.

On Friday after school we all went home as fast as we could and did what we had to do and then we sneaked away and went to the stop sign where the school road meets the Post Road. Willie and Henry were there already and I could see Klaviera and Alma coming when I got there. Penzel and Jakie soon came with their bikes and then Emmie and Trudy hurried up. Ronnie came shooting with his slingshot. We stood there a little while and all of a sudden we saw a bicycle coming from the village road and soon we could see that it was Emmanuel and when he a little bit closer was we could see that he had a brand new bike. We started to sing: "Happy Birthday to you! Happy Birthday to you! Happy Birthday, dear Emmanuel. Happy Birthday to you!" And we were all waving our hands and the boys waved their caps and then he stopped by us. He had a carrier on his bike and it was full with a box that had a big drink bottle sticking out from it. Emmanuel was smiling like it was the best day in the whole world and he led us across a flax field till we were by these trees in the middle of the field on a little bit of hill.

Emmanuel got off his bike and led it into the trees till we came to the middle where it was like a room with a roof because the branches were closed at the top. There was a pile of wood and lying beside it were some willow sticks, sharp at one end. Emmanuel took the box out from his carrier and set it down on the ground. Then he took some matches out from his pocket and he lighted on the fire. Soon it was burning good and he opened the box and gave everyone a weiner. Just when he was giving me mine, we heard something in the trees and it was Judy. "Where were you?" Klaviera wanted to know and Judy got a little bit red and she said, "I had to take the eggs out," and Emmanuel gave her a weiner, too.

So we had a nice weiner roast. Emmanuel had brought two weiners for everybody and buns, too, with relish and mustard already on and two big bottles of Orange Crush so we could drink from them. It sure tasted good and everybody was so happy and Emmanuel went around to see that we all got two weiners and two buns and something to drink. When the hot dogs were all finished he pulled a bag out of the box and gave us marshmallows to roast.

"Jesus Fuckin' Christ!"

Forscha and his herd came hopping out from the trees and Forscha had his Rifleman air rifle and he started to shoot into

145

the fire and they went running around and hitting our marshmallow sticks into the fire and saying Jesus things. Emmanuel asked them if they wanted some marshmallows and Schuzzel threw the whole bag in the fire. Little Willie started to cry and Melvin slapped him on the mouth.

All of a sudden Melvin had Emmanuel by the arm and was twisting it behind his back. Then Johnny had my arm and I saw Judy take Klaviera and hold her. Forscha stood there with his air rifle and Schuzzel and Abe stood across from him so that nobody could run away. I tried to wriggle away from Johnny and Forscha shot me on the shoe with the BB gun and it sure hurt.

Forscha walked over to Emmanuel and spit in his face. "Jesus Murphy!" he said. "You should wash your face!" And he slapped his cheek with his hand.

"The other one, too!" Melvin laughed. Forscha slapped him again.

"Tie him on by that tree!" Forscha took the braided rope that he had hanging from his belt. Melvin marched Emmanuel to a sugar tree that was quite straight and put his arms around it. Forscha tied his hands, then winded the rope around Emmanuel's chest and the tree. Emmanuel didn't say nothing. He just looked up to the tops of the trees.

Forscha spit on Emmanuel's face again. Melvin spit, too. Then Johnny and Schuzzel and Abe.

"Now everybody!" Forscha yelled. "Everybody spit on Jesus!"

Nobody moved. Johnny twisted my arm and pushed me to Emmanuel.

"Spit!"

I didn't. He twisted harder. Abe hit me with his hand in the balls. It hurt so much that I started to cry, and I spit. Emmanuel didn't even move his eyes.

Then the others had to spit. Penzel and Willie. Jakie and Ronnie. Henry, Trudy, Alma, Emmie. Judy pushed Klaviera in front of Emmanuel.

146

"Spit!"

Klaviera didn't spit. Judy pushed Klaviera's face right into Emmanuel's.

"Spit!"

Judy's hand reached up under Klaviera's sweater and she pinched her. Klaviera screamed, but she didn't spit. Judy spit instead.

Shuzzel started to sing: "Jesus had a weiner roast, weiner roast, weiner roast. Jesus had a weiner roast and we all spit on him."

"Let's see if Jesus has a weiner!"

"Yeah let's!"

Forscha went over to Emmanuel and spit on him again.

"Does Baby Jesus have a weiner?"

He reached Emmanuel between the legs and started to feel him around through his pants.

"Oh, oh, I found something. You want to see it?"

"Yeah! Yeah!" Forscha's gang shouted.

"Yeah! Yeah!" Judy shouted.

"Do you want to see it?"

Johnny's hand was me between the legs and he squeezed. Tears started to run. "Yeah," I said.

Forscha went to Klaviera.

"Do you want to see it?"

Judy's hand was still under her sweater.

"Yeah! She wants to see it!"

Forscha went back to Emmanuel.

"They want to see it. Klaviera wants to see it."

He opened Emmanuel's belt buckle. Then the button on his pants. He pulled down the zipper. His hand reached in.

"Oh, oh, I found something. It's nice and warm. And a sack, too. Two warm eggs."

Emmanuel jerked his head like he couldn't help it.

"Oh sorry. Did that hurt?"

Forscha pulled his hand out and held it under his nose.

"Phew it stinks! Jesus, don't you ever wash yourself?"

Forscha pulled Emmanuel's pants down. Then the underpants.

"Look at that. Jesus has a weiner!"

Forscha pulled the skin back.

"Look how stiff it is. Come and feel it."

Abe and Schuzzel felt it first. Then Melvin grabbed Willie and Penzel and made them feel it. And then he moved the skin back and forth a few times. Abe grabbed Alma and made her touch it. Schuzzel pushed Emmie and Trudy close and they quickly touched it and turned away. Johnny gave me a knee from the back and shoved me over and I touched it. Emmanuel just looked up and he still didn't say nothing.

Everybody touched it, even Klaviera. Judy pushed her to Emmanuel. Klaviera started to fight and she almost got away, but Forscha grabbed her, too. They pushed her to her knees in front of Emmanuel and Forscha reached her hand out to touch it.

Then my tongue is cold. My jaws still move like I'm trying to tell something. But no shtimm comes out. Then it slowly seepers into my head what I'm still trying to say, how it really was in my pants that day and I look at Forscha Friesen and I don't want to hammer any more nails, not even into myself.

Klaviera starts to play on the piano "Just as I am without one plea" and I feel real light in my head and I turn from the pulpit away and start to go to the steps and I have left my Bible on the pulpit but I don't turn back for it and I feel like I have hooked loose a whole hayrack load of junk by the mist-acre and the tractor is driving in road gear, home at last, and my shoe hooks on the top step and my ankle bends and then I am head under heels on the floor.

"Yasch! Yasch!"

"Huy Yuy Yuy!"

"Knibble Thiessen come!"

Then Oata is holding my head and Muttachi is pulling off my shoes and then the rightmaker is rubbing my feet.

Chapter Nine

A woman can sure do lots of things if you only give her a chance. I mean, just look at Oata there driving that 27 John Deere combine like she was born on it. And her father always complained that his fat daughter couldn't do nothing right. For sure Nobah Naze would never have had to hire an oabeida if he had just let Oata do a few things. I mean, I only showed Oata how to drive the combine because she said she almost fainted while she was shovelling off the grain by the auger so I figured things would go faster if Oata could drive the combine a little while I shovelled. At least then we shouldn't have to hold up the thrashing each time the hopper was full. But now I can't get Oata off the combine, she likes it so much. And it's her combine so what can I do? I sit in the truck waiting for her hopper to fill up and I drive the half-ton to the yard and load off the grain with that old auger that has the motor tied together with binder twine.

Yes sir, Oata has come a long way since Nobah Naze died. Who would have thought only two months after her Futtachi went dead that she would be driving the combine all herself and that she would have engaged herself with me, Yasch Siemens the dow-nix, and be going with me every Sunday to church and *me* making a testimony by the Christian Endeavor and everything? But then who would have thought that fat Oata Needarp who we always nerked in school would have gotten a catsup bottle full with chokecherry wine from out of the cellar and made me forget that I was heista kopp in love with skinny Sadie Nickel? Well, such a thing you never really forget all the way, but for sure Oata has made me to see things different, like maybe it's not so bad to do things that other people do, like go to church and get married and be a farmer.

That's the best part, being a farmer. With my own land. Well, Oata's land and her mother's, but her mother is in the mental home and I mean the land will be as good as mine, at least after we've gone to stand the preacher in front in the spring when I have learned the catechism and let the eltesta pour water over my head.

It's pretty good really, watching Oata handle that combine. I sit here in the half-ton with a straw in my teeth and I feel like I'm in a cartoon that I saw in the *Cooperator* once about the olden days when people only had a little bit fur to wear for clothes and this man has these two women pulling the plow for him. Well, in farming you do what you have to to make it all work, and I am thinking that if Oata is so good with driving combine that means we shouldn't ever have to hire a helper to get the work done in the busy seasons.

Still, I wish Oata would let me drive the combine sometimes. Driving a big outfit, like a tractor or combine, now that's farming. A person feels real strong standing on a 4010 John Deere pulling a big CCIL disker or a twenty-foot John Deere deep tillage cultivator. Yes sir, when you turn that rig around at the end of the field and your hands and your feet smoothly move the brakes and the clutch pedal and the hydraulic lever and the throttle and you feel those shovels sink into the ground and the diesel puffs black from the muffler when the shovels are in a little too deep so you pull back to make it just right, well it's almost like it is with Oata when she is feeling her oats and won't let me go home for night. Mind you, Oata's 27 John Deere combine isn't exactly a big rig and her old Fordson Major tractor is no Versatile four-wheel drive. But it's a start and anyways it's the land that's important. I mean, a guy can have a big outfit but if he doesn't have a field to plow, what's the use?

But it bothers me a little bit when I come to Oata's place this morning and she is already with the grease gun by the combine pumping all the zirks full.

"Yasch, you go milk the cows. I have to change oil and clean the air cleaner yet!"

Change oil and clean the air cleaner? What knows a woman about that? And milking cows? Well for sure that is the woman's job, especially at thrashing time when the man should be busy keeping the combine fixed ready and stuff like that. On a farm it's supposed to be fifty-fifty—the woman works in the house and the barn and the man works with the machinery on the field. But what can I do? It's still Oata's place and I guess if she wants to do the man's work she can. I mean if I wasn't engaged with her she would have to do it all herself anyway, or hire somebody. So I milk the cows.

"Fry some eggs for breakfast!" Oata calls when I bring the milk out from the barn. "I'll be in to eat soon." Well, okay, I think to myself, just today, but for sure this isn't the way it's supposed to be.

So I'm picking egg shell out of the eggs in the frying pan when Oata hurries herself into the house and goes straight to the phone.

"A sprocket has some teeth broken out," she says as she cranks the phone for the operator. "I'm phoning John Deere

Derksen to see if he has a new one." I put Oata's eggs on her plate and I hear her say, "Good, I'll come pick it up this forenoon."

Oata starts to eat her eggs and I say, "Maybe I can pick up some beer. It would sure taste good after a hot thrashing day."

"Oh you don't have to come with. I can find John Deere Derksen's place easy myself. Somebody has to wash dishes and feed the pigs and chickens yet."

"Wash dishes?" I don't believe what is coming to my ears.

"Yeah, they haven't been washed for two days already. I have to go." Oata hurries herself outside before I can even say anything more.

Well, I start to get dizzy. I mean it seems like something is turning the wrong way here. *I* should be getting the parts and *she* should be washing the dishes. I think maybe we should start having devotions and reading the Bible by breakfast time so that Oata can learn herself that the man is supposed to be the boss in the house.

I feed the pigs and the chickens. Then I look at the combine where Oata has taken the sprocket off. I think maybe I can finish changing oil for her but it is finished already. I go around with the grease gun but every zirk has lots of grease, even the one I sometimes forget. The air cleaner has fresh oil and is wiped clean. The gas tank is full.

I look at my watch. I put gas in the auger motor and change the oil. I clean the spark plug. I start the motor up. It runs okay but I play around with the timing screw anyway. In the pasture I see the cows jumping on each other and I think I should maybe call Henry the bull, but Henry will be thrashing, too, and I don't think he would come. I clean out the little bit manure from the gutter in the barn and tickle the calf's ear. I pump full the water trough. Then I sweep out the granary that I swept out already last week. I go back in the barn and check to see if all the lights are working and I change one bulb in the hayloft that was burned out already last summer when I worked for Nobah Naze.

The sun starts to get hot. I see Hingst Heinrichs's truck driving on the mile road and it turns in by Ha Ha Nickel's. And I wish I was there again, working by Ha Ha Nickel's and playing catch with Sadie in the evenings. But that can't never be now. Sadie and Pug Peters are having a hurry up shroutflint wedding next week. So sticks the fork in the handle.

I am starting to get a little bit hungry when I see the dust from the '51 Ford coming down the road.

"Did you make dinner?" Oata calls when she jumps out of the car with the new sprocket in her hand.

"No," I say. "I didn't know when you were coming."

"Well, hurry go make something while I put the sprocket on. The forecast says rain for tonight!"

"No, you go make dinner. I can put the sprocket on." I reach for the sprocket and Oata swings herself away.

"No! I'll put it on and you go make dinner!" I reach for it again and Oata swings the sprocket with her arm and almost cuts my nose off. "Go make dinner!" Then Oata is bending over a little bit, drops the sprocket and holds her stomach with her hands.

"What's loose? Oata, what's loose?"

"Nothing. Just go make dinner." Oata picks the sprocket up and turns to the combine. So I go to the house wondering maybe if there was some egg shell in the breakfast and she swallowed some and has a stomach ache.

Well, making dinner doesn't hurry itself so easy because I have to wash some pots first before I can cook something and that old range takes so long to make the water hot and then I have to figure out something to cook and the potatoes have to be peeled yet and the knife doesn't want to cut the baloney and the water in the pot doesn't want to boil. When Oata comes in the potatoes are still so hard that you can hardly stick the fork in and the baloney is burned black in the pan.

"How come you didn't wash the dishes?"

"Didn't have time."

"Get some buns and jam. We don't have time to wait. You can fry the potatoes for supper."

So goes it then. Oata drives the combine, I load off the grain and make the faspa and cook the supper. We use the last clean dish. The rain holds off till two in the morning and we finish the field. I think tomorrow Oata will have time to wash the dishes.

I stand up a little bit late and when I get to Oata's place the '51 Ford is gone and Oata has put a big sign on the house door: WASH THE DISHES. Well, holem de gruel. What does that woman think this is? I mean Oata should like to be in the house washing dishes and listening to "Back to the Bible" and "Heart to Heart" on the radio. What's loose with that? So I don't even go into the house. Instead I do the barn chores and measure how much grain is in the granary and stuff like that. But by dinner time Oata isn't home yet so I go to Muttachi's to eat. While I'm driving my half-ton down the muddy road it all of a sudden falls me by that maybe I can ask Muttachi to come wash dishes and cook for us during thrashing when we are so busy. I mean everybody needs help at thrashing, so Muttachi could easy come over for a while and work for us and then we wouldn't have to worry about who will wash the dishes and cook.

But Muttachi doesn't think at all that it's a good idea for her to come and wash Oata's dishes. "What you think I am?" Muttachi says from the table where she is sitting with a cup of tea and a carrot and one small bun. "You think I will stick my nose into Oata's business? No way."

"You wouldn't be sticking your nose in her business. We just need some help now while we're so busy with thrashing."

"Who's thrashing today in the rain, huh?"

"Well...."

"How come you can't wash your dishes today when you're not thrashing?"

"Well, Oata went to town today and we don't have any...."

"So what's loose with you, you're not crippled! Why can't you wash the dishes?"

"But Muttachi, that's the woman's job."

"Who says it's the woman's job?"

"In the Bible it says the man is supposed to be boss in the house."

"Then go be boss in the house and wash your dishes!"

"But Futtachi never had to wash dishes at our place."

"Sure he did. Not very often, but he did. You were just too young to remember."

"Hey, is that all there is for dinner?"

"That's all I need. The doctor said I don't need to eat so much."

"Well, make me something, I'm really hungry."

"Go pull a carrot out of the garden and wash it off for yourself."

"No, I mean cook something!"

"Yasch, let me say you something. Twenty-three years I cooked for you and wiped your narsch. Now you're getting married I quit. I don't need to cook dinner for myself and I won't cook it for you. I will not come your dishes to wash. Besides, Shaftich Shreedas are taking me with to visit some people by New Bothwell so I don't have time to wash dishes for lazy people."

I'm really bedutzed now. My own Muttachi telling me that she won't make me something to eat and that she won't come to help me and Oata. It sounds like it's maybe the second coming or something. Maybe I should go to Preacher Janzen's place and tell him that it must be the end of the world. But my stomach is hanging crooked and it's growling and I know I have to go back to Oata's if I'm not going to die from hunger. I am flat broke so I couldn't even go to town to eat.

Oata isn't home yet and it's raining harder again so there isn't much that a person can do outside. So I go in the house and eat the last baloney with some buns and mustard pickles. I try to reckon out when I ever saw my Futtachi wash dishes or cook something and I'm thinking through when I was young and the things I can remember about my dad and all I can remember is about the time me and him cut pigs together. We had waited till the pigs were too old and five of the little boars died and that was the first time I ever knew that Futtachi hated to cut pigs even if he was doing it for all the neighbors. And I think about one other time when my Futtachi was very important to me, that time when I was nine years old and we were living in town because Futtachi was building the new elevator and the Brunk Tent Crusade came to the fair grounds and everybody went every night to hear the preaching, even Futtachi sometimes, though he was tired from building the elevator all himself, and this one night the preacher preached real loud and long and I was real scared that for sure I was going to go to hell because I was bad all the time and I had to try real hard not to let the tears come when they were singing "Just as I am without one plea" and the song is sure one to grab on to your tears, especially when you don't know what a plea is except that for sure you know you don't have one. When they had hummed it about ten times I just couldn't stand it no more, so I grabbed Futtachi's hand and he squeezed mine and I looked at his rough fingers and the thumbnail that was black from where he had hit himself with the hammer and the hand seemed so strong and big like maybe I could crawl all the way into it and then for sure no devil or satan that a Brunk Tent Crusade talked about would be able to hurt me and I held on to Dad's hand all the way home to that little house by the train tracks. And I wasn't scared one little bit.

My head reckons even farther back to the time when we still lived by Yanzeed. I was still very small when one night Futtachi woke me up and said we had to go to the hospital because Muttachi was going to get a baby. We drove into town and stopped by the hospital where there were lots of lights on and Futtachi said I should stay in the car and he took Muttachi into the hospital. I went to sleep in the car and then Futtachi came back alone and he said that Muttachi was going to stay there for a while and that was when Futtachi washed dishes. He didn't leave them for Muttachi to do when she got home. Even a few days later when Muttachi came home and there was no baby along and Futtachi said the hospital didn't have one fixed ready for us and Muttachi just went to bed and she stayed in bed for a long time, Futtachi was almost all the time cooking and washing dishes and I can't remember that he ever complained that he had to do women's work. When he finished washing dishes he played with me checkers on that old board with checkers sawed off from a broomstick.

So I'm sitting in Oata's house listening to the rain on the windows, smelling the dirty dishes, and I hear again my Muttachi say that for twenty-three years she cooked for me and wiped my narsch and for sure Muttachi is right like Muttachis always are. I feel real small. I look at the cupboard and the dishes. I get up, switch the range on and heat up a pail of water.

So I wash those dishes and it's not easy when the food has dried on for three days already, but I keep rubbing and scratching till I at least can't see no more dirt on them. And it doesn't seem like such a bad thing what with listening to the radio and looking out the window at the rain. Still it is almost time to do the chores when I finish.

I am creamering the milk when Oata comes home. She walks into the house very slowly. She is wearing her pink dress and looks like she's been crying.

"Oata, what is loose?" I ask quietly.

Oata doesn't say nothing, just sits down by the table. She doesn't look at me.

"Oata, where have you been? What's wrong?"

The clock ticks. Oata looks at me, then past me. "You washed the dishes!"

"Well, for sure. Somebody has to be boss in the house around here."

Oata smiles a little bit. "Sit down," she says. I sit down at the table across from her and put my hand on her hand. My hand is clean white from washing dishes and her hand still seems to have some grease from the oil change around the edges of her fingernails.

"Yasch, we will have to get married right after the thrashing is finished."

"Okay, but I thought we would marry ourselves in the spring."

"We can't wait that long."

"Why not?"

"Yasch, I'm going to have a baby."

"What?"

"I'm going to have a baby."

"A baby?"

"Yeah, a baby. So I don't think we should wait till spring to get married."

I don't know what to say. I mean for sure such things will happen when you stay for night, but well you just don't think that, well I mean it's just that how is a person to believe that such a thing could really happen, that that is really the way it's done. Sure a person knows all that but I mean you never know really that that is really cross your heart true. Oh shit, I'm just all mixed up.

"Yasch."

"What?"

"Are you mad at me?"

"Mad at you? What for?"

"Well, uh, well we have to get married early."

"For sure not. I mean we were getting married anyways."

"Will it bother you what the people will say?"

"What people?" I squeeze Oata's hand.

"Well, all the people."

"Oata, the only people that matter is us. If we let other people bother us we will never be happy. That's how we are." Then I remember that I still have to take the blue milk to the pigs. When I get to the door I think of something else. "Uh, Oata, now that you are having a baby does that mean you can't drive combine no more?"

Oata laughs. "Yasch, just because I'm going to have a baby doesn't mean I'm crippled. I can still drive combine. For sure it's easier than washing dishes."

Chapter Ten

Did you ever have a day when you couldn't get nothing done because it seemed like nobody wanted to mind their own business? Just one bother after another? Well today it seems like it is such a day. Me and my boy, Doft, he's twelve, are trying to get the manure shovelled out of the pig barn and so far we haven't filled up the manure sled even once. First Oata comes to get the car keys from me so she can go to the store, which shouldn't take very long, but she has to tell me first what all she heard on the radio before she came to the barn and one of the things is that there will be a Progressive Conservative meeting at the Gutenthal curling rink next week Tuesday. Oata has just hardly driven off the yard when little Frieda, who is seven, comes from the house and says somebody is phoning for me. So I go to the house and it's some lawyer outfit that wants to take away a farm from a guy called Siemens because there is a receivership on it. So I tell him that my land doesn't even have a rowboat leave alone a receivership. He swears on the phone and says, "Am I speaking to Jack Siemens?" "For sure not," I say. "I'm Yasch, not Jack." And he wants to know how he can get a hold of Jack Siemens. So I tell him about the six Jack Siemenses I know and that if he is mixed up with Jake Siemens there are about seven more at least and four yet that write themselves 'Jac.' but I don't think any of them have ships on their land, but old J.J.P. Siemens in Prachadarp was born on a ship coming from Russia so he was a Canadian before the rest of the family. And I tell that lawyer that I'll send him a bill for the information.

When I get back outside Hingst Heinrichs stops in the yard with his Ford truck that has custom cab, CB and mag wheels. When he climbs out I see that he is wearing one of those Farmers Revivalist caps like you can see on TV. I didn't know that the caps were brown and white because me and Oata still watch that old 11-inch black and white that I got cheap from Ha Ha Nickel when he had to buy himself a color set. Some people around here now have booster cable TV and Ha Ha Nickel's son-in-law Pug Peters has one of those dishwasher TV things in his yard that they say can get 200 stations.

Anyway, Hingst tells me that there will be a meeting by the Elks Hall in town next week and that every farmer that doesn't want the family farm to disappear should go to that meeting. I look at him and wonder what he means by a family farm when he has three sections all himself and it says 'The Hingst Heinrichs Corporation' on his truck. But I just say, "I figure my family farm is okay!" Hingst looks at me. "Yeah, I guess you would say that." I know he is thinking yeah sure, Yasch, you married yourself a farm so it didn't cost you nothing. I know he is thinking that and it's true. I married myself with fat Oata Needarp after her father Nobah Naze died and I am farming a half-section all paid for and even some money in the bank. And Hingst says that even if I figure I'm okay I should come anyway because it looks like maybe the bank is going to try to close Pug Peters's farm and at the meeting farmers are going to decide if they can stop the bank. "In tough times," he says, "we have to stick together." I smile a bit and say what Shaftich Shreeda said when he ran for the NDP: "When the going gets tough, the tough get going." And I say that if I get my manure shovelled out of the pig barn I'll come to the meeting. Hingst laughs. "Yasch, you cheap bugger. Why don't you build a decent pig barn with an automatic barn cleaner?" I just look at him and say, "Like I said, my family farm is okay."

Hingst Heinrichs isn't away five minutes when Yut Yut Leeven's boys, Laups and Lowtz, drive in the yard. I say to Doft, "It's a good thing I'm a Flat German all full with *Wehrlosigkeit* otherwise I would stick these guys with the pitchfork already," because Laups and Lowtz can spread the bullshit as good as a Better Bilt Honey Wagon. But Laups's wife is pretty good friends with Oata and I mean I used to spread a bit of manure with these guys too, in the Neche beer parlor where we would see all kinds of Flat Germans drinking beer that didn't want to be seen in the parlor at home. Yut Yut Leeven used to be the biggest farmer in Gutenthal and Laups and Lowtz would never let you forget it. I used to be scared of them when I was small because they were so rich and I was just a poor boy weeding beets by their place. But after I had weeded beets there for three weeks I wasn't scared no more. I guess you could say we are friends. The Leevens aren't the biggest farmers no more, like the brothers only have a section and a half between them. Sure, they got their farm from their Futtachi, so it didn't cost them so much, but I don't know if it was something that Yut Yut told them when he was living his last days in hospital or if the Leeven boys are smarter than everybody else. Maybe it's because they were well off when they were young so it didn't seem so important when they were older. But that time when we went to Laups's cabin by Mouse Lake, me and him went fishing early in the morning. We didn't catch anything but we had a long talk in the boat and Laups said to me, "You know Yasch, in this world a man has to decide how much he needs to live on, and then be satisfied with that. How much farm does one man need?" And I was thinking to myself, yeah sure, it's easy to say that when you have all you need already, because I had an application in to borrow myself money to buy Pracha Platt's half-section. But the Credit Committee from the Credit Union said no. They said I didn't have enough farming experience and not enough equipment for so much land. The next week I found out that Ha Ha Nickel had bought Pracha Platt's farm for his son-in-law, Pug Peters. Well for sure, I was pretty mad about that for a while, because I was once quite a bit crazy about Ha Ha Nickel's skinny daughter Sadie, but she let Pug Peters get into her first and now he got the land that I wanted.

But Pug he hailed out that year and I had a good crop even if I could hardly get the thrashing finished because that old 27 John Deere combine just didn't want to work any more. Still the price of wheat was good so I bought myself a newer Massey for almost all cash and I didn't have to go in the hole to keep farming. I was farming 100 pigs, too, not in a fancy barn with a manure pit and all kinds of fans, just the ordinary old barn. Sure it's hard work but at least a person can make a bit of money and so what if some of the neighbors complained that my pigs were stinking up all of Gutenthal. I know what money smells like. I put the manure on the fields, too, so I didn't have to buy myself fertilizer with borrowed money and the next year when that old Fordson Major tractor needed an overhaul I bought myself a 4010 John Deere that Puch Panna had traded off on a Versatile four-wheel drive. I got a good deal because no farmer wants such a small outfit no more.

Still I wanted to be a bigshot farmer and when Fuchtich Froese got sick and had to sell his three quarters I tried to buy, at least one quarter, but the Bank of Commerce manager wouldn't give me a loan except if I got somebody to co-sign for me. So I just went and got a case of beer instead. That was the year before little Doft would have to go to school so me and Oata were talking about it all and we had never gone for a trip when we got married so at Christmas time I shipped all the pigs and we slaughtered the chickens and I borrowed the cows to Zoop Zack Friesen for a month and we went to Florida.

Sure, Yasch Siemens isn't a bigshot farmer like the others, but it's not so bad really. With only a half-section I can really farm it, and I don't think I have any more wild oats and mustard than the neighbors who use all that Avadex BW and Hoe-grass stuff they show sliding on a curling rink on TV. In the winter time I read things about organic farming and I don't know but for a small outfit like mine it seems to work. A farmer always has worries but it sure doesn't seem so bad when you don't have to worry about feeding the bank manager's family, the lawyer's family and the implement dealer's family. But then Oata helps, too. She makes a big garden and we have our own chickens, pigs, cows and things so we hardly even have to worry about feeding the storeman's family yet, too. Doft sometimes wants to know how come he can't have one of those games that you play with the TV like the neighbors' boys have but I just laugh and say that while those guys are playing with themselves on TV he can play with their girlfriends.

Anyway, I'm running out of the furrow here with this story. Laups and Lowtz Leeven come by the yard and they are both laughing like crazy when they climb out of the cab.

"Hey Yasch, did you get your mail today?"

"No, Oata is getting it."

"Look what we got."

"Yeah, look." Lowtz holds out a small card. I take it from him. It is a membership card for the Gutenthal Progressive Conservative Party and it has Lowtz's name written on it and is signed by Haustig Neefeld who is president for the Gutenthal PCs.

"I got one too," Laups says and shows me his.

"Two timers," I say. "Bunch of two-timing Liberals."

"Now now Yasch. Don't be so fromm. I'll bet Oata will bring you one from the mail, too. It seems like everyone in Gutenthal got one, even Shaftich Shreeda!"

"So who is paying for all this? That macaroni baloney fella?"

"Maybe it's Clark's pork 'n beans," Lowtz says.

"Nobody knows for sure, except that Puch Panna said that Haustig Neefeld said that last week he got all these membership forms in the mail with money to pay for the cards. So Yasch, I bet Oata will bring you home a Conservative card."

"Well, Yasch, it won't be so bad. I mean you already have a blue Sunday suit."

Sure enough, Oata drives in the yard and right away holds up the PC card with my name on it. "Yasch, Yasch, what is loose with you? Did you give money to these penzels without asking me?"

"No, no Oata. You think I would throw money away? Everybody in Gutenthal got one in the mail, even drains like these guys here."

"Oh, and here I thought maybe some screws were getting loose in your head. Do they have lunch by these PC meetings?"

"Oh sure," says Lowtz. "Haustig Neefeld's mumchi and Fuchtich Froese's daughters have been making lunch already for a whole week."

"Good, then we can go to the meeting. If you can eat free, why not?"

"That's the stuff, Oata. We'll see you at the PC meeting."

The Leeven boys drive away and Oata goes in the house. I stand there looking at the PC membership card, trying to figure out why they would want to have me for a member, especially when I have always voted for the NDP. And the reason I vote for the NDP is because when I was thirteen I was heista kopp in

166

love with Shaftich Shreeda's daughter Fleeda. And Shaftich Shreeda was the only person in Gutenthal who had the nerves to vote for the NDP and tell other people about it. He was voting for the NDP when most of the Flat Germans still voted for the Social Credit and the NDP had only changed from the CCF a little while. Sure, there were lots of jokes about the Canadian Common Fools and the Cooperative Cow Fornicators and then when it changed to NDP they said No Damn Policy. But then it seemed like the Gutenthallers got tired with Social Credit. It seemed like it could only work if you had lots of oil wells and those that talked the loudest about More Debt or Social Credit moved themselves away to BC. So in Gutenthal people voted P C again because they figured it had been so good with Honest John Diefenbaker. I vote NDP because with Shaftich Shreeda's daughter Fleeda was the first time in my life that I was heista kopp in love and even after Fleeda went off to be a missionary and married herself with somebody in Africa and it's all water through the culvert now, it warms me up a little bit to vote for the NDP. My wife Oata never tells me who she votes for. She says it's nobody's business, it's like why you have a door on the beckhouse.

It's been pretty good being married with Oata, what is it now, twelve years. That's how old my boy, Doft, is and Frieda is seven. The ball team laughered themselves good when we got married a little bit in a hurry. I mean, we didn't even wait for the preacher to have time, we just went to the judge in Emerson and got married there. I think it was just as good as in the Gutenthal church. At least we didn't have to feed everybody buns and baloney in the church cellar after the wedding. Yeah, they laughed when I married myself with fat Oata Needarp and the guys on the ball team were marrying themselves with all kinds of thin women. But now their wives are all pretty fat and my Oata is still slowly getting thinner. It happened while she was in the hospital with little Doft and she was reading in this

167

States magazine about a woman that was even fatter than Oata and how she got quite thin. Oata sneaked that magazine home from the hospital and she didn't even tell me nothing about it. She started doing the stuff that was in the magazine and very slowly she started to get thinner. I mean it was going so slowly that I didn't even notice it really, you know how it is when you live with a person every day for years, you forget to look real close, until that time when Doft was six years old and Frieda was one, Laups Leeven and his wife, Tusch, invited us to come for the weekend to Mouse Lake and before we went there Oata drove to town and when she came back she called me upstairs into the bedroom. She was dressed up in a bathing suit and it was like I had never seen Oata before and I said to her that we would have to leave the lights on at night some time. Oata poked me where my belly was hanging over my belt and said, "You think I want to look at that?" Sure, Oata isn't skinny like Sadie Nickel, who after three kids is still thin like she was fifteen, but if they ever have a Mrs. Gutenthal contest I will sure enter my Oata.

I guess you could say that I'm one of the still ones in the land. After I got married with Oata I stopped to pitch for the ball team. I don't know, but it seemed like one part of my life was finished, that the ball team was something I didn't need no more. I haven't even gone to look at the ball games but now Doft is twelve and he has been asking if he can go so maybe I will start again. I've been teaching Doft how to be a pitcher and he likes it, but it seems that now when the kids go to school in town they don't get the same chance to play baseball like I did in the Gutenthal school. I'm a still one in church, too. Sure, me and Oata go to church every Sunday like most others here. It's a good place to rest after a week's hard work. But after I gave that testimony one time nobody has asked me to do anything more.

I hardly even go to the curling rink in winter. When they first built it I curled two winters but when a man gets older it just seems like dummheit to stand on the ice when it's thirty below and freeze your feet. Besides, now that they have artificial ice in town they didn't even make ice in Gutenthal last winter and those only that are all stone in the head would want to curl from before thrashing is finished till seeding time like they do now. No, I'm not one of those that is always away at meetings for this and that. I vote when there is a vote and that's it.

Still, now that I have a Conservative card it bothers me. There it is on a piece of paper, my name, connected up with politics. Sure it must be a joke, but when your name is on a piece of paper it can lead to all kinds of things. I just feel like something will happen. I try to shove it out of my head and think only about getting the barn clean. Doft has been doing most of the shovelling while my head has been driving all over the place. I am proud about my boy Doft. He is strong and does good in school. When he was being born I was sitting in the waiting room in the hospital sweating because it was taking Oata so long and I was alone there. It was the middle of the night and I was worrying about Oata and about me, wondering if I was strong enough to be a father. And I was thinking about what kind of a person I was and I could only see all the bad things about myself, how lazy I was, and all the times I went to drink beer with the ball team, or that time on Halloween when lots of flax straw bales were burned. Or that time me and Hova Jake picked up Susch and Tusch from Sommerfeld and said we are going to hear Barry Moore in Dominion City but instead went driving around and did lots of things that Barry Moore probably preached against. Yeah, I gribbled about all this till my shirt was as wet as it gets at haying time but in the end the head straightens it all out and the nurse came to tell me to come look at my boy.

In Saturday's mail comes an announcement about the PC meeting. It says that the guest speaker will be Yeeat Shpanst. That's all it says. Yeeat Shpanst. It doesn't say who Yeeat

Shpanst is or where he is from or what he will talk about. Well, I figure maybe the real PCers know who he is, I mean nobody knew who Joe Clark was neither. And I think to myself that maybe it would be nice to have a good Flat German in the government, except that it always seems like the Flat Germans that get in the government always pretty soon forget that they are Flat Germans and when you see them on the CBC news they sound just like a radio, not like maybe they weeded beets or shovelled manure when they were young.

Anyway on Sunday we are driving to church with the kids and all of a sudden Doft says, "Hey Papuh, look at that there on the hydro pole." I look and stop the car. There stapled on the pole just like you always have when there is a vote is a poster that says YEEAT SHPANST—TOMORROW'S LEADER-SHIP TODAY. I look down the road and see that every other pole has a Yeeat Shpanst sign.

"Huy Yuy Yuy," Oata says. "Maybe we should rip some off to take home for starting the fire in the stove." She pokes me in the ribs with her elbow. Those signs are every place. On the side of Pracha Platt's old barn there are a bunch of signs stapled to make the letters Y S.

Walking the church in it seems like everybody is fuscheling about Yeeat Shpanst. I take a bulletin from Forscha Friesen who has never figured out anything else to do with himself after all these years and sit down. Even in the bulletin under announce-ments it tells about Yeeat Shpanst's meeting at the Gutenthal curling rink.

Well for sure on Tuesday evening the Gutenthal curling rink is full with people. So full that they have to move the meeting out from the waiting room to the ice part. It's a good thing some-body thought about bringing a loudspeaker system because usually at the curling rink you don't need one for a meeting. At least not if only the Gutenthallers come but it seems like every Flat German between here and Yanzeed has come to Gutenthal. And lots of English and French too it seems like.

At eight o'clock Haustig Neefeld stands up, goes to the mike and starts to tell us what this meeting is for, that it is to pick those people who will go to Ottawa from Gutenthal to pick the new PC leader who will for sure be the next PM. For sure that's what the country needs, a PCPM, and Fuchtich Froese who is sitting there in the front starts to clap but the people don't clap, they start to shout, "We want Yeeat Shpanst!" And it looks like Haustig Neefeld doesn't know what to do, because for sure I'll bet he doesn't know who Yeeat Shpanst is any more than I do. So he stands there letting the people shout and he drinks some water and he still doesn't know what to do till Fuchtich Froese stands up and fuschels something in his ear. Then Haustig Neefeld lifts his arms up and spreads them out like wings holding his palms down and he shakes them up and down till the people get quiet and he says in a voice that squeaks a little bit like he is maybe telling a lie, "Ladies and Gentlemen. I give you Yeeat Shpanst!" Clapping and whistling and shouting for about five minutes and nothing happens. Then all of a sudden it feels like the people are making room for somebody in the middle of the rink. Everybody gets still. Then somebody is standing there in front by the mike. A short man, maybe five two, with a big baseball farmer cap on. He lifts his arms and points the visor of his cap to all the four corners of the curling rink. I hear a bobby pin drop out of Oata's hair. It sure is still. The man leans close to the mike.

"Welcome to the nineteen eighties!" You can hear five hundred people swallow their spit all through the rink.

"Welcome to this packed meeting!" Someplace one hand claps.

"Welcome to Yeeat Shpanst country!" Two hands clap.

"Welcome to Gutenthal!" A thousand hands clap, but quietly like if we were maybe in church.

"Ladies and Gentlemen. The bottom line, at this point in time, is between a rock and a hard place. Irregardless—irregardless of how you are politically orientated there's no doubt that the powers that be—the powers that shall no longer be—have impacted on every aspect of our lives with it's metrificated Intrudo policies that are turning good people into confused objects of pity. Like my neighbor who was filling out a long government form last week and he had to convert all his bushels into litres and his acres into what-the-hecks." Somebody coughs. Somebody laughs a bit.

"Exactly. The trouble with our country today...." He stops and sips a bit of water. "The trouble with our country today is that our government in Ottawa is like a beetweeder that hacks off all the beets and leaves the weeds standing, then says, 'Look how well the crop is growing.' I say that it's time to let the government know that it is buttered out!" We clap now. Buttered out is good Flat German.

"Seriously now...." We still clap. "Thank you, thank you...." We clap harder. "Seriously now, the number one issue in the country today is the arrogance of incompetence that has turned our mighty Parliament into a house of ill repute—a common bawdy house!" We clap a little, but now we are a little nervous. I mean, should a Flat German talk like this?

"My friends, I did not come here to lick your recessionary wounds. In the past few weeks you have been inundated by known and unknown quantities asking for your support. Ladies and Gentlemen. I'm an unknown quantity, too. That's the monkey on my back. But it's the unknown that this country is yearning for in these troubled times. Who needs a track record —of derailments? Just consider the facts. This great party has been leaderless now for three months, and yet the polls show that our party has the highest popular standing in history. This is no time to cut our losses—just our losers. It is time to be forging ahead! The future is up for grabs! It is no time to back off!

"We must end this dramatic stalemate. We can no longer tolerate government by budget leak. Fellow Canadians, I stand before you offering to lead.

"But I am not alone. Others make the same offer. You deserve more. You deserve a real alternative. It has been said many times that there is no real difference between the two main parties in this country—except for arrogance. I propose to change all that.

"What this country needs is a new vision. I was born on a Manitoba sugar beet field. My earliest memories are of my dear mother's cracked and calloused heel as I learned to crawl along a row of beets. I lived in the granaries with the beetweeders. Yes, my native brothers, I was there with you. I watched my mother destroy the weeds. I watched the point of the hoe blade slip between double plants to cut off one so the other would have room to flourish. But look at the field today. The weeds grow alongside the beets, and whenever the beets get a little ahead of the weeds the government pumps more fertilizer on the weeds and when that isn't good enough it sends in Revenue Canada with hoes to cut down the best plants to give the weeds a better chance.

"I have a vision—I see millions of beetweeders with hoes sharpened descending on our choking fields, hacking away at the mustard and the wild oats, separating the doubles, freeing the sweet sugar beet to flourish as we weed our way into the future. There with the help of God I will lead you!"

And then before the people can even start to clap, Yeeat Shpanst shouts out that we should all sing "Oh, Canada" and that his campaign manager will lead us and a tall man in a blue suit jumps up beside him and starts to sing and it only takes one line before I know and everybody else knows that the singer is Hova Jake! Hova Jake whom I haven't seen since he went away to Rosthern College to school and then we heard one time that he was singing with a born again disco band. Well, for sure "Oh, Canada," sings hartsoft good.

For the next month Gutenthal is not the same. There are raffles, mission sales and collections to send Yeeat Shpanst to the leadership in Ottawa. All of a sudden it seems like he is relatives with almost everybody and he talks on CFAM and CISV and then one day he is even talking on CFRY. The *Echo* and *The Times* and *The Carillon* all have pictures of him and long write-ups about what he says in his speeches. And always his meetings are packed with people, especially after Hova Jake brings along a quackgrass band that sings Flat German songs. Every evening we all watch *The Journal* to see if they will have heard of Yeeat Shpanst yet but it seems like Barbara and Mary Lou only know about the people whose initials are BM or JC, and when one of those JC guys makes it sound like the JC should remind us about a fisher of men, well the Gutenthallers think for sure that Yeeat Shpanst is the right man.

Haustig Neefeld, Fuchtich Froese, and Penzel Panna are the delegates from Gutenthal to Ottawa and seven days before the convention they crawl into one of those Triple E camper vans with Yeeat Shpanst and Hova Jake. Before he closes the door Yeeat says to those seeing him off, "In seven days we will change the world." Off they drive, and each day we listen to the radio and look at the television to see if we can hear about them, but there is nothing. Nothing at all. And we figure, well they'll be on TV for sure Friday night when all the candidates are supposed to make speeches. We all watch the TV on Friday night. And all the candidates make their speeches, but not Yeeat Shpanst. Nobody says even one word about him, not one word. We watch the TV till our eyes are sore trying to see the Gutenthallers someplace in the corner of the screen, and we think maybe we should have had another raffle so the quackgrass band could have gone along and for sure they would have gotten on TV.

Saturday all day, watching the TV. Sunday nobody goes to church in case something comes up on the TV, but nothing, nothing about Yeeat Shpanst. Not one person holding up a Yeeat Shpanst picture on a stick, not one. Where is he? Where are Haustig Neefeld and Fuchtich Froese?

174

I think maybe Penzel Panna got lost in a beer parlor because his wife isn't along to lead him by the nose.

So the PCs vote in somebody else, it doesn't really matter, and the Gutenthallers are thinking they should vote Social Credit again. I figure I'll just stick with the NDP. Monday afternoon Ha Ha Nickel gets a phone call from the Winnipeg airport to see if he will come to pick up Neefeld, Froese and Panna. So Ha Ha picks them up. Yeeat Shpanst and Hova are not along. The three men don't want to say nothing about what happened.

But one day I see Penzel Panna in town and I talk him into sneaking in the beer parlor with me and he tells me that the first thing that happened when they got to the convention was that Yeeat and Hova saw this hartsoft beautiful woman and somebody said that she writes for a newspaper. Yeeat and Hova right away went to her and said who they were and how they came there with the Triple E van and everything. So she said she would like to see the van to write about for her newspaper. They went outside to the van and the other three men were hungry and helping themselves to some sandwiches on a table. When they finished eating they turned to look for Yeeat Shpanst but they couldn't find him, even when they went back to the parking place. The van wasn't there. They walked all up and down that garage, all twenty floors, but no van. All day Saturday and Sunday neither Yeeat nor Hova showed up and that hartsoft beautiful girl that writes for a newspaper didn't come back neither. Haustig Neefeld found out from another newspaper man with a funny name like Fudderingham, or something like that, that the hartsoft beautiful woman's name was Barbara, only it's not the Barbara from TV because she still comes on *The Journal* almost every day.

So I've got my seeding done and the fields are greening quite nice. The bank closed up Pug Peters's farm and had an auction sale. Hingst Heinrichs and the Farmers Revivalists wanted to do something about it and I even went to their meeting to say what I thought they should do: "Don't buy nothing at the auction sale!" Well, at the sale it seemed like that was the way it would be for a while, but then one guy saw what a good deal he could get there on a new swather so he started the bidding and before the day was over it seemed like just about everybody had bought something except me. Even I almost put in a bid for Pug's television dish but then I thought that if I brought home a $2000 antenna they wouldn't be satisfied with that 11-inch black and white no more and be after me to buy color, and that's just too much. In these troubled times you have to watch out.

Books by Turnstone Press

George Amabile **Ideas of Shelter**

David Arnason **50 Stories and a Piece of Advice**
The Icelanders
Marsh Burning

Sandra Birdsell **Night Travellers**
Ladies of the House

George Bowering **The Mask in Place**

Dennis Cooley (ed.) **Draft**

Frank Davey **Surviving the Paraphrase**

Ed Dyck **The Mossbank Canon**

Patrick Friesen **The Shunning**
Unearthly Horses

Gary Geddes **The Acid Test**

Steve Johnson & David Landy **The Folk Festival Book**

Daphne Marlatt **How Hug a Stone**

George Morrissette **Finding Mom at Eaton's**

George Ryga **Two Plays**
Portrait of Angelica and A Letter to My Son

Steven Smith **Ritual Murders**

Andrew Suknaski **Montage for an Interstellar Cry**

Wayne Tefs **Figures on a Wharf**

Geoffrey Ursell **Traplines**

David Waltner-Toews **Good Housekeeping**